The Dangerous Voyage

The Dangerous Voyage

Gilbert Morris

BETHANY HOUSE PUBLISHERS
MINNEAPOLIS, MINNESOTA 55438

Cover illustration by Lino Saffioti

Published by Bethany House Publishers
A Ministry of Bethany Fellowship, Inc.
11300 Hampshire Avenue South
Minneapolis, Minnesota 55438

Printed in the United States of America.

Library of Congress Cataloging-in-Publication Data

Morris, Gilbert.
    The dangerous voyage / Gilbert Morris.
       p.   cm.
    Summary: Trapped in the year 1620 after a trip in an
experimental time machine, fourteen-year-old twins Danny and
Dixie set sail for the New World on the Mayflower and discover
some surprising things about the faith and life of the pilgrims.

    1. Pilgrims (New Plymouth Colony)—Juvenile fiction.
[1. Time travel—Fiction. 2. Mayflower (Ship)—Fiction.
3. Pilgrims (New Plymouth Colony)—Fiction. 4. Massachusetts—
History—New Plymouth, 1620–1691—Fiction. 5. Twins—Fiction.
6. Brothers and sisters—Fiction. 7. Christian life—Fiction.]
I. Title. II. Series: Morris, Gilbert. Time navigators ; 1.
PZ7.M8279Dan   1995
[Fic]—dc20   95–9620
ISBN 1–55661–395–4   CIP
                                           AC

To Zac Morris—
My grandson and good buddy!

GILBERT MORRIS is a prolific writer who has consistently topped the best-seller charts in the Christian market. A retired Professor of English who earned a Ph.D. from the University of Arkansas, he brings both his love of history and his affinity for adventure to the pages of THE TIME NAVIGATORS. His family includes three grown children, and he and his wife make their home in Alabama.

1

"WHY WOULD YOU WANT TO VISIT those two old crazies?"

The bus ticket agent stared at Danny Fortune in amazement. The fourteen-year-old began to wonder whether his plan to visit his twin great-uncles was such a good idea after all. He had secretly traveled to Mayville by bus after school, hoping to get a chance to speak to them in person. Now, seeing the agent's reaction, Danny wished he'd never stopped to ask for directions. "Well . . ." he began, not sure what to say.

Cocking his head, the ticket agent leaned forward and peered straight at Danny. "If you really *want* to go see them, you'll have to walk or take a taxi. They own that creepy-looking gray house about two miles south on Highway 123. But I'm warning you, most folks don't have anything to do with those guys." He turned away from the counter, leaving Danny looking after him nervously.

I wish I'd never seen that newspaper clipping! Danny thought as he slowly made his way up the driveway. The big gray house was set back in a thick grove of towering pines. When his mother had showed him the article about his wealthy great-uncles earlier in the week, a secret visit had seemed like the perfect solution to his family's money troubles. But now that Danny was actually walking up the steps to the front door, he wished he were back home. He saw a heavy rope hanging down in place of a doorbell. When he pulled it, he heard a hollow clanging deep inside the house.

If Danny hadn't been so nervous, the old building would have intrigued him. It looked like something he'd seen in movies about haunted houses—three tall stories with spiraling turrets and huge draped windows.

The door swung open with a groan. Danny jumped back, startled by the large form that appeared. A gigantic man loomed over him, his imposing figure filling the entire doorframe. "What do you want, boy?" he grunted.

Danny felt his knees go weak at the sound of the gravelly voice. He eyed the giant's banana-sized fingers and gulped. "I'd like to see the Fortunes, please."

The doorman glared down at Danny with a pair of small, piglike slits. He moved as if to slam the door when a voice called out, "Who's there, Toombs? If he's selling something, tell him to go away!"

Seeing his chance, Danny ducked under the giant's arm and slipped into the house. A very short man with a thin white beard and deep-set black eyes stood staring at Danny in alarm. "No boys living here!" he said loudly. "Get out of my house!"

"But . . . I've come such a long way to see you, Mr. Fortune," Danny explained as Toombs grasped him by the collar and started to drag him out. "Please—can't I talk to you for just a minute? I'm Danny Fortune—James's son!"

"Wait a minute!" the little man shouted. He stared at Danny with piercing black eyes, his expression suggesting that he was thinking of something unpleasant. "Let him go, Toombs. Come with me, Danny!"

Danny squirmed loose from the giant hand and followed the short man up a winding staircase. At the top, they entered a huge room packed with books from the floor to the high ceiling. In the center of the room was the biggest desk Danny had ever seen. It was almost hidden beneath the mountain of books, papers, and magazines that covered it. A head popped up from behind the mountain as they entered the room. It belonged to a man with the same sharp black eyes and dark complexion as the man in the white coat. Danny knew he had found the other Fortune twin.

"What's this?" he asked in a high voice. "You know I can't be interrupted, Zacharias!"

"I know, I know, Mordecai," his brother said soothingly. "But I think you ought to meet this young fellow. You remember James—our nephew? Well, this is his son, Danny." Zacharias gave Danny a quick smile that didn't reach his eyes, saying in a friendlier voice, "I'm your great-uncle Zacharias—the noted inventor, I might add—and this is my twin Mordecai, a distinguished historian."

He seemed to be waiting for Danny to say something, but now that Danny was here he couldn't think of where to begin. Finally, Mordecai cried out impatiently, "Well! Why are you here, boy? We haven't got all day, you know!" He was wearing an old suit that had been blue once, but now was so shapeless and faded it resembled a sack. He nodded his head up and down with his every word, as if to punctuate them.

"Now, Mordecai, be patient!" Zacharias gave his brother an odd look, and Mordecai's expression suddenly changed. It was as though a silent signal had passed between the two brothers. "I'm sure Danny would feel more comfortable if we could find him a place to sit down. Let's have a little something to eat while we get acquainted."

"Good idea!" Mordecai agreed. He lifted his voice and called out, "Teenie! Please bring us some cakes and tea!"

Danny soon found himself relaxing as the two men entertained him with stories of their unusual work. By the time an elfish old woman brought in a tray of cakes and tea, he was able to talk. "I realize you've never met me before, but I know my dad worked for you some-times when my family needed the extra money. That's kind of why I'm here."

The twins shifted in their chairs and glanced at each other uncomfortably—they seemed to sense what was coming.

"A week ago, my dad left our apartment to pick up some papers at his office. We haven't heard from him since." Danny swallowed hard and looked blankly at the stacks of expensive leather-bound books that filled the room's deep shelves. He still couldn't believe that his father had vanished.

"My mom is out of her mind with worry. She just doesn't know how she's going to be able to support us if Dad doesn't come back soon—especially when my little brother Jimmy needs regular medical attention." Danny looked up at Zacharias and Mordecai. "He'd die without his treatments." The two nodded sympathetically.

Why, this is going to be easy! Danny thought with a feeling of relief. "Anyway," he said, hurrying to finish his story before the mood of the odd pair changed, "if you could just give us a *little* help, we'd really appreciate it."

The room was quiet for a moment. Zacharias thoughtfully stroked his beard. "Well, Danny, my boy, I'll admit that your story touches me. After all, blood is thicker than water, isn't it, brother Mordecai?"

"I don't know about that!" his twin responded. He got

up and began pacing and waving his hands in the air. "People have to learn to stand on their own two feet. They shouldn't go begging from anybody—family included!"

"That's exactly what my mom has always said," Danny said quickly. "Why, she just won't take charity!"

"Ahh!" A slow smile crept over Mordecai's face. "Well, if *that's* the case, we might be able to do something for you."

"Really? That's great! We'll pay you back." Danny could hardly believe his good luck. Maybe there was something to Jimmy's prayers.

"No need to do that, Danny. All we ask is a little—" Mordecai hesitated, then gave a short laugh. "A little *service*, shall we say?"

"I'm willing to do almost anything!"

Mordecai rubbed his hands together and looked at his brother. "He could be a promising prospect, eh, Zacharias?"

"Yes, indeed!" Zacharias agreed enthusiastically. He got up from his chair. "Follow us, Danny." Danny followed the two men downstairs to the first floor, then down another flight to a mammoth basement. Rows of fluorescent lights lit up the windowless room, which was crammed with dozens of weird-looking machines. A large, glass-domed contraption making strange whirring sounds filled up the middle of the room.

Danny's mouth dropped open in surprise. "Wow, what's that?"

"Ah!" Zacharias smiled and pulled him closer to it. "Do you like it? *This* is simply the most important thing in the scientific world, Danny!" He paused and proudly added, "This is the Chrono-Shuttle!"

Inside the clear machine, two chairs were positioned

in front of some kind of monitor. Wires laced through the glass tubing that wrapped around the back of its dome, which glowed with an eerie green light. As Danny moved closer to get a better look, a strange warmth began to radiate from the shuttle.

"So what exactly does a Chrono-Shuttle do?" he asked skeptically.

Zacharias put his hand on Danny's shoulder. His eyes gleamed. "You must *never* tell a soul what I am going to tell you. Promise? I know your father was a good man; he kept his word! No matter what happens, do you promise never to say a word about what you are about to witness?"

"I . . . I promise!" Danny wasn't sure why the pair were suddenly so secretive. They'd been in such a hurry to show him the machine.

"Very well," Zacharias nodded. "What you see before you is an invention that I have spent my entire life perfecting. It is like nothing the world has ever seen! With this machine, Mordecai and I will be able to uncover the mysterious secrets of the past. And once we do *that*, the future will be ours!"

Danny looked hard at the machine, not quite understanding. "But . . . what does it actually *do?*"

His great-uncle pointed dramatically at the Chrono-Shuttle, then whispered, "Why, it's a time machine, boy!"

Danny stared at the Chrono-Shuttle in disbelief, then turned his gaze on the two men who were regarding him carefully. "Is this a joke?"

Zacharias laughed unpleasantly. "You think I'm some sort of a mad scientist, don't you, Danny? It's only natural, I suppose! But I can give you a demonstration that will resolve all your doubts." He walked over to a wire cage, opened a door, and pulled out a white guinea pig. "This is Ronald," he said, holding the animal out to Danny for a moment of inspection. He then opened the shuttle door and placed the animal on the seat. Walking to the large control panel stationed beside the machine, he put his hand on a lever. "Now, keep your eyes on Ronald, and I'll show you how this thing works!"

Zacharias pulled the lever down, and Danny kept his eyes fixed on Ronald. At first nothing happened. Then there was a humming noise that filled the room and seemed to shake the entire house. The green glow grew more intense, and a little ring of white light appeared around Ronald. The guinea pig seemed to be vibrating!

For a split second, Ronald became blindingly white, as if he were filled with light. And then, just as suddenly, he vanished.

Danny gaped in astonishment at the spot where the animal had been. "Where—where did he go?"

"By my calculations, Ronald is now in the year 1666," Zacharias said after consulting the control board in front of him.

"Probably in the middle of the Great Fire of London," Mordecai added, peering over his brother's shoulder at a digital readout. "Better be more careful where we send our next guinea pig, I guess." He shrugged his shoulders. "Come over here in front of the board, Danny, and I'll show you how this thing works.

"There are two problems to time travel—both of which we have solved. First, there is always a danger if you go back in time of materializing right in the middle of a solid object. One misplaced landing, and you're stuck forever! We solved this problem by developing a sensor that prevents you from materializing inside a solid in the first place. A brilliant solution, I think. Now, see these two buttons? They control your location. This one is for latitude and the other is for longitude. That way, you can not only go back in *time*, but you can go back to any spot on earth!"

"And *this* is the control pad for time," Zacharias added, pointing to something that looked like a digital clock. "You simply set it to the date you want, and *boom!* You are instantly transported to that time period!"

Danny could hardly take in everything his great-uncles were telling him. The whole scene was like something out of a science-fiction movie. "But how does it work?"

Zacharias gave Danny a wilting look. "It has taken me a lifetime to develop the shuttle. Do you really expect to understand it in five minutes? But then, you don't really need to *understand* it. All you need to do is *travel* in it!"

Suddenly, Danny understood the meaning behind the twins' covert glances at each other. These two men wanted him to be their human guinea pig! He thought of Ronald and immediately backed away from the two, protesting loudly, "No way! I'm not going to get in that thing!"

"I thought you said you'd do *anything* to help your family!" Mordecai reminded him. "Well, here's your chance. The Chrono-Shuttle is not dangerous—though I will admit it looks rather menacing."

Zacharias reached under his white coat and pulled out a fat billfold. Opening it, he took out a thick wad of bills and began counting. "Let's see—I have about—oh, about five thousand dollars here—for a start." He looked at Danny and smiled. "Would that help your mother, Danny?"

Danny stared at the huge roll of bills. It was so much! Taking it would mean they could pay for Jimmy's treatment bills. There might even be a little left over!

The offer was awfully tempting, but one thing kept niggling at him. "But where's the guinea pig? Tell me that. Money won't help my family at all if I'm stranded back in year one!"

"Goodness, Danny! Surely you don't think that your own relatives would endanger your life? Why, that would be unthinkable!" Mordecai acted offended. He picked up a small, thin round object off the table next to him. It looked much like an old-fashioned silver pocket watch. Danny studied it closely, noting that it had several tiny dials and a slight bulge in the middle.

"Here, you see this bulge? Release it—like this—and you have a button. This little device is your ticket back to the present, Danny. It's really much too complicated to explain, but we call it the 'Recall Unit.' When you want to come home, just push that button. The control computer here will respond, and—flash!—you're right back here with us in our own time!"

Danny thought quickly, then asked, "If it's so easy, why don't *you* do it?"

"Nothing would please me better," Mordecai sighed. "I'm a *historian*, Danny. Zacharias designed the Chrono-Shuttle for me so I could find out the truth about our past. I don't want to rely on the fables we have today. Take all those stories about the Pilgrims, for instance. Why, historians have made William Bradford and all the others who settled at Plymouth out to be a lot better than they actually were! They came to America for financial gain, not religious freedom! And I intend to expose them!" His eyes lit up with pleasure, and he went on, "But unfortunately, I must remain in the present due to a small heart problem I have. No excitement, the doctors say. And of course, Zacharias can't go, since he's the only one who can control and repair the shuttle."

"How do you know it will work? Has anyone ever actually gone back in time?"

"Well . . . yes, and it worked fine, except—"

"We *did* have a technical problem once, when the machine was still in the developmental stages," Zacharias added quickly. "But that's all been overcome. Nothing can possibly go wrong now!"

He put his hand on Danny's shoulder, and Mordecai came around to his other side. Their dark eyes shone with a strange, hungry light. Danny pulled away, angry at their scheming. "I'm not about to become your guinea pig!" He ran for the door, fully expecting them to try and stop him, but they didn't.

As he raced up the stairs to the front door, he heard Zacharias calling, "You'll come back, Danny. I know you won't let your family suffer!"

Danny zipped right past Toombs and into the open air. He kept running down the road as fast as his feet would carry him, until finally he was sucked dry of air. Exhausted, he sat down, dragging in great gulps of air. When he could breathe again, he got up and trudged back toward the bus station.

As Danny walked, he thought about the strange experience he'd just had. Once, he kicked in frustration at a rock that got in his way. He hated to feel pressured by anyone, least of all by those strange men. There was no way he was going to accept their crazy offer! *I should never have gone to see those two in the first place! If only there were another way. . . .* But try as he might, Danny could not think of another plan to get the money his family needed so desperately.

2

"YOU'LL COME BACK, DANNY. I know you won't let your family suffer!" Danny stood in front of his family's battered apartment door, trying to erase the words that kept playing over and over in his head. If only he could forget that he even had any great-uncles!

He raised his hand to knock, then hesitated, struggling with the anger he felt every day since his father had disappeared. Danny knew Zacharias and Mordecai were only trying to help, but they just didn't understand how big a risk he would be taking by accepting their offer. *What would Mom do if I disappeared too?*

Danny still found it hard to believe that it had only been a week since his dad had vanished. So far, the police search had failed to turn up even a trace of him. The last few days had been especially hard, as the few leads they'd had resulted in dead ends. Danny's hope was all but gone, and he was growing angry. Life without his father just seemed impossible!

Angry tears pricked his eyes, but he shook them away and knocked on the door. "Who is it?" his younger brother called out. By the time Danny answered and the old door creaked open, he had managed to plaster a smile on his face.

"Danny!" Jimmy cried, his dark blue eyes enormous in his thin face. "Did you bring the book?"

"Sure did! Did you think I'd forget?" Danny pulled a small library book out of his pocket and handed it to the eager five-year-old. Jimmy could barely wait to get his hands on it. "I haven't seen this one yet! Thanks!" he said, heading at once to his bed to lie down, already engrossed in the pictures of dinosaurs.

"He's been real good, Danny," Dixie reported as she came out of the kitchen to greet him. It was her night for supper duty. "Mrs. Jones said he ate most of his lunch and took a nap." Dixie was Danny's twin. She was only two inches shorter than his five feet ten inches, but she seemed a lot shorter because she was always stooping.

"Straighten up, Dix," Danny said automatically. His sister's self-conscious habit really got on his nerves sometimes. To his amazement, she burst out crying and ran to the sofa. Burying her face in the worn pillow, she sobbed uncontrollably. Danny stood still in surprise for a few seconds, then ran over and yanked at her arm. "Dixie! What's the matter?"

"Nothing! Leave me alone!" came her muffled voice.

"Aw, come on, Dixie," Danny persisted, uncomfortable with the situation. "What's wrong?"

Dixie sat up, jerked a tissue from her jeans pocket, and wiped her face. She looked at him and asked, "Danny, do you think I'm ugly?"

He opened his mouth to say she wasn't half bad but changed his mind. "Ugly? Of course you're not ugly! You'd have to be decent looking to be related to me!"

Dixie was actually quite pretty, he realized. Like him, she had big blue eyes and thick auburn hair, but her hair managed to stay in place instead of sticking up like his. Sure, she was a little taller than most girls, but she wasn't too skinny as she'd been a year or so ago. Of course, she *did* have crooked teeth. He gave her a quick glance, noticing that she held her mouth tightly closed, another habit she'd formed in the last few months.

Dixie still looked doubtful, so Danny smirked and tried again. "Don't worry, Dixie. An orthodontist could have those fangs fixed in no time!"

Dixie jumped up and glared at him, her tears flooding back. "Quit being such a creep, Danny! You know we'll never have the money to pay for braces now!" She dashed out of the cramped apartment, slamming the creaky door behind her.

Feeling guilty, Danny walked slowly into the kitchen. He knew Dixie was right. The Fortune family had never had enough money. Jimmy's medical bills ate up nearly all of his dad's paychecks, and now there might not be any more paychecks to count on. He glanced into the pan Dixie had abandoned on the stove. "Macaroni again! I'm so sick of the stuff I could. . . !" His appetite gone, he went into the tiny bedroom he shared with Jimmy to check on him. Plumping down wearily beside his younger brother, Danny asked, "Want me to read you a story?"

"Yeah! Read the one about the boy with the sling-shot, Danny. I *like* that one!" Danny picked up the worn book of Bible stories from the table and began reading. He knew the story so well that he watched Jimmy as much as he read the words on the pages.

Seeing Jimmy's condition made Danny even more depressed than he already was. Jimmy had cystic fibrosis, and he seemed to get thinner and weaker all the time. He never complained about the painful treatments, but Danny knew they were hard on him. Mostly, the Fortunes tried not to think about Jimmy's future. Especially now that James Fortune was missing.

Danny heard the door close as he wound up the story. Had Dixie returned? "Why don't you look at your library book while I finish making supper."

"All right, Danny." Jimmy was never one to give his brother trouble.

Danny found Dixie standing over the stove, staring down at the lumpy macaroni. Her eyes were red and swollen. "Sorry I teased you, Dixie," he began. "You really are a pretty good-looking girl—for a sister."

"It's okay, Danny."

Neither one said anything more, but it was all they needed. The two had discovered long ago that they understood each other much better than most brothers and sisters. Twins were often that way. No matter how successfully they covered up what they were feeling from others, they couldn't hide much from each other. Even Dixie's few words told Danny that he was forgiven.

But as they worked together to set the table, he knew full well that she wasn't *really* okay. Her teeth were still crooked, and there wasn't any money to get them fixed. They were not going to straighten on their own. He remembered the thick roll of bills Zacharias had held out to him. *It would be kind of fun to travel back in time,* he thought. *But can I really trust my great-uncles?*

Ellen Fortune had not come home yet, so her three children decided to go ahead and eat without her. They gathered around the table, and it was Jimmy's turn to ask the blessing. He liked to pray so well that he stretched it out, giving thanks slowly and carefully over everything on the table—including the knives and forks! When he was through, Danny grinned and reached over to rub his head. "You sure have a lot to pray about!"

"Well," Jimmy replied, a serious look on his face, "we've got a lot to be thankful for."

Danny glanced at Dixie, who bent her head and started shoveling in her food. "What's the rush?"

"I've got to hurry," she mumbled, her mouth full. "Promised to study with some of my friends."

"Oh? Which ones?"

Dixie avoided looking at Danny as she answered. "Just a couple of girls from my math class. I don't think you know them."

Danny said nothing, but he knew she was hiding something. Dixie finished eating and got up from the table. "Would you do the dishes for me tonight? I'll do them tomorrow."

"Sure," Danny agreed. "Don't stay out too late, or Mom'll worry."

"I won't," Dixie promised as she went out the door.

As Danny washed the dishes after putting Jimmy to bed, his mind wandered back to Zacharias and Mordecai. Should he tell Dixie about his visit? He'd never tried keeping anything from her before—he didn't even know if he could. Then again, it seemed to him that Dixie had her own share of secrets lately. He had heard from one of his classmates that she'd started hanging around with a pretty wild crowd. If she could keep secrets from him, then surely he could keep one from her!

Danny was just sitting down to his algebra homework when he heard a key in the lock. Springing off the couch, he met his mother at the door. "Did you learn anything new at the police station?"

Ellen Fortune shook her head and brushed a wisp of blond hair out of her blue eyes. She looked pretty even when she was exhausted. She reached out to give her son a hug, and he gave her a hard squeeze in return. "Hey!" she halfheartedly teased Danny, who was just as tall as she was. "Watch out for your poor mom's back!"

Danny laughed. His mom had always had a good sense of humor. "We saved you some macaroni. I can reheat it for you if you want," he offered. Mrs. Fortune nodded and went to her bedroom to put her things away. By the time she came back in her worn blue robe, Danny had her supper ready.

His mother sat down at the table and sipped at a cup of coffee. "Where's Dixie?"

"Out studying with some friends. She should be back soon."

"And Jimmy? Was he all right today?"

"Yeah. Ate all his lunch and had a good nap." Danny stirred uneasily on his chair. He knew his mother hated to be away from them at night, but the rent was due soon, and the extra hours she was putting in at work would really help out.

Mrs. Fortune traced the rim of her cup in silence, her eyes sadder than they had been since she had first learned her husband had disappeared. After what seemed like a very long time to Danny, she finally spoke.

"I've stopped by the police station every night, just hoping that they might have some news about your father. They never do. I'm starting to wonder whether the police alone are ever going to be able to find him." She kept her eyes on the table, as she sometimes did when she was struggling not to cry. Danny's stomach knotted up inside. He wanted to jump up and run out of the room. Instead, he waited for her to continue.

"If we had the money, I'd hire a detective—someone

who could do the job right. I'm thinking of taking a second job anyway, to help out with Jimmy's medical expenses. Maybe there'd be something left over for a detective." Mrs. Fortune raised her eyes to meet her son's, and Danny nodded reassuringly.

"Are there any relatives who could help us out—give us a loan or something?" he asked a little timidly. He knew that his parents hated to owe anyone money. If only he could help! Was traveling in the Chrono-Shuttle really the only way?

A tear rolled down his mother's cheek. It was the first time Danny had seen her cry since his father had vanished.

"You know that your father and I were brought up to take care of ourselves, Danny. When we got married, we agreed that we'd never count on anyone but each other. And that's what we've done." She looked out the window at the glow of the streetlights, and a smile touched her face—as if a very nice memory had come to her. "A lot of our friends took all the help they could, but not us. We wouldn't even take help when your dad was a graduate assistant at Penn State!

"But now . . ." she whispered, looking down at her empty coffee cup. "I don't know—maybe I'm being selfish."

Danny squirmed. He hated to see his mother like this. "What about asking for a loan? We'd pay it back. Don't we have *any* relatives who could help?"

"My parents were all I had, Danny, and they died in a car wreck before I was married. Your dad doesn't have any either . . . except . . ." She paused and looked out the window.

"Mom?"

Mrs. Fortune came back to the present. "Well, your father *does* have those two uncles—the ones mentioned in the clipping I showed you—but I don't think they'd help. I tried to get hold of them when your father disappeared, but they haven't answered. Anyway, there's always been something funny about them."

Danny thought back to the peculiar little men with their white beards and odd clothes. His mother would be alarmed if she knew just what those two were up to!

"Even though your father did odd jobs for Zacharias and Mordecai, they've always treated us very strangely," his mother continued with a frown. "Still, as an associate history professor, your dad and Mordecai had a lot in common. He went to see them not too long before he disappeared." She sighed and got up from the table. "I doubt we'll get any help from that corner." Mrs. Fortune switched off the kitchen light as she headed to her bedroom, leaving her older son alone in the dark.

Danny lay awake for a long time that night. His mattress seemed lumpier than usual, and the thought of his rich great-uncles kept going through his mind. There really didn't seem to be any other way to get the money his family needed. Finally he decided.

"I'll call them first thing tomorrow. I've just *got* to do something!" He closed his eyes, feeling more hopeful and excited than he had all week.

3

DANNY SAID NOTHING TO ANYONE about his plans to visit the great-uncles in Mayville. He tried to put his upcoming adventure out of his mind as he struggled through classes the next day, but he couldn't. The more he thought about it, the more scared he felt. His overactive nerves made him edgy and short-tempered, and he began to wonder whether he shouldn't let Dixie in on his secret.

It was after lunch that things got really out of hand. Danny was sitting in history class half asleep as Mrs. Simpkins droned on about how some country had gone to war with some other country when a monitor came from the office with a note. Mrs. Simpkins looked at it, then said, "Danny, Mr. Watts wants you in his office."

Danny got up, ignoring the usual comments students made when someone got called to the principal's office. The last thing he needed today was a trip to see Watts!

When he stepped inside, Mr. Watts, a short fat man with a jolly face, was not jolly at all. He gave Danny a funny look and said, "Danny, I got a call from your mother. She wants to see you right away."

"Is it about my dad, Mr. Watts?"

"I don't think so."

"Well, I'll go right home."

"Your mother's not at home," Mr. Watts said, then

hesitated before continuing. "She's at the police station."

"What's she doing there if it isn't about my dad?" Danny stared at the principal in confusion.

"It's Dixie," Mr. Watts said. "She's in some kind of trouble." He gave Danny a concerned glance and added, "Your mother said she was caught shoplifting."

Danny was stunned. "That can't be right, Mr. Watts! Dixie never stole anything in her life!"

"Maybe it's a mistake," Mr. Watts suggested, but he sounded unconvinced. "Come on, I'll take you over to the police station. Your mom's waiting for you there."

The ride over seemed terribly long. Danny couldn't believe that Dixie would do something so stupid. What had gotten into her? When they arrived at the police station, Danny stepped out of the car. His mother was waiting inside. She was sitting on a bench, and Danny saw at once that she'd been crying.

He ran over to her, asking, "Mom? What's happened?"

"Dixie took some jewelry from a store." Mrs. Fortune twisted a tissue in her hands and lifted her eyes to her son's. "I want you to be with me when I talk to her—you understand her so much better than I do."

Inside at the front desk, a heavyset, red-faced woman took their names. "Go down to Room 210," she instructed. "Officer Keller is there with your daughter now, Mrs. Fortune."

They hurried down the hall. A voice called, "Come in," when Danny knocked on the door of the office. Entering, they saw Dixie sitting on a chair, her face white as paper and tear marks staining her cheeks. The policeman beside her was a tall, thin man with a face lined with deep wrinkles. He stood up.

"Mrs. Fortune? I'm Officer Keller. Why don't you two take a seat." Once Danny and his mother were settled, he began, "First of all, let me tell you that no charges have been filed. Dixie isn't under arrest. The owner of the store was very understanding—I think he could tell that it was Dixie's first attempt."

The officer kept on talking, stressing that this first offense had to be the last if Dixie was to be helped. Dixie kept her eyes on the floor and sat there silently, seemingly frozen with fear and shame. She had obviously been crying, but Danny thought she looked more angry than scared.

At last they were able to leave the police station, but only after making an appointment for Dixie and Mrs. Fortune to report regularly to a court official for three months. When they arrived at home, Jimmy was still awake and playing with Mrs. Jones. Not wanting to upset him, they waited until after he had gone to bed to talk.

Dixie had refused to eat supper. She stared blankly at the door, her face empty of any expression.

"All right, Dixie," Mrs. Fortune broke the silence, "I'd like you to tell me why you took those things."

Danny expected Dixie to scramble to excuse what she'd done, but instead she looked her mother right in the eye and said stiffly, "I took those things to sell them for money to have my teeth fixed."

"But, honey, it wasn't right," Mrs. Fortune said quietly. "You've been brought up to know better than that!"

"I don't care how you think you brought me up!" Dixie returned, her eyes sparking. "I'm so *ugly*! What difference does it make if I'm a thief too?"

Mrs. Fortune and Danny tried to calm her down. For over an hour they argued, but Dixie would not budge. She clamped her lips shut and shook her head stubbornly.

But Dixie's experience wasn't the only thing that ruined Danny's evening. After Dixie finally went to bed, Danny's mother dropped another bombshell while they washed the evening's dishes. "I didn't want to tell you this yet, but we've got to move."

"Move! But why?"

"Our lease is up soon, and the manager told me this morning he's raising the rent. I just don't know how we can afford to stay here without your father's income. This isn't much of a place, but it's probably better than what we'll have to take." She started to say more, but her lips started trembling, and she quickly pressed her fist to her mouth and turned away.

Danny watched her shaking shoulders and whispered, "Mom, please don't cry! It'll be all right somehow. I promise." For a moment his mother stood perfectly still, then she whirled and ran out of the room, leaving Danny alone—and more worried than ever.

All night long he tossed on his lumpy bed, thinking, *I've just got to get out to see Zacharias and Mordecai tomorrow! It's the only way!*

Danny stumbled absently through school the next morning. *I need to go back to Mayville tonight*, he told himself. *But first I've got to tell Dixie what's going on— just in case something happens*. He managed to catch up with her at her locker, but she ducked her head and tried to get away.

"Dixie, we've got to talk."

"I don't want to talk about it anymore, Danny," she said wanly. Her face was pale and she looked tired.

"Not about yesterday. It's something else," he said. "Let's go down by the pond." She followed him reluctantly to the old concrete fish pond in front of the Federal Bank two blocks away from the school. They sat down on the concrete lip and watched the huge goldfish—some of them red, some yellow, some mottled in various colors. He tried to think of a good way to begin, but nothing came to mind. Finally he pulled his shoulders together and started in. "Dixie, we've never lied to each other. What I'm going to tell you sounds like something out of a movie, but it's the truth."

She sat there looking down at the fish swimming in slow motion as he began to talk, but soon her eyes were riveted on his face. When he finished, he said, "Well, that's what happened. Do you believe me?"

"Of course," she replied instantly. "And I know why you're telling me." She put her hand on his shoulder. "You've decided to do it, haven't you?"

Danny exhaled slowly. "I think it's the only way, Dixie. I'd get down on my hands and knees and beg if I thought it would work! Our great-uncles have got so much money, and it would only take a little—"

"Let's go right away!" Danny could tell Dixie's brain was already busy making plans. "Mom said she wanted to go spend the day with Marion Terry, and she's taking Jimmy with her. You know how he likes to play with her little boy."

"I don't want *you* to go, Dixie!" Danny said, alarmed.

He shook his head, adding, "Those two are a pair of weirdos—and their butler looks like Frankenstein's monster!"

But Dixie ignored him, and despite his protests, they did just what she'd suggested. Danny told their mother they were doing some late work at the library, feeling only a little twinge of guilt at the lie, and the pair of them repeated Danny's journey—taking the bus into town and then walking the two miles out to the old house.

"It looks more haunted than ever," Danny muttered as they walked up the steps.

"Oh, I think it's *romantic*!" Dixie whispered. "It's like a house in an old movie!"

When Toombs opened the door, the scene was almost *too* "romantic" for her. Dixie flinched as his huge body filled the door. Danny felt sure she would have run if he hadn't been there. Toombs leered at them and bellowed, "They're waiting for you—down there."

Danny nudged Dixie, whispering, "Come on." Hanging back a little, she followed him down the dark stairway.

"Well, well—I'm glad to see you again—and I see you've brought your sister too," Zacharias said with a smile. "Come in, my dear! My name is Zacharias, and this handsome fellow is my brother Mordecai."

Dixie gulped and mumbled faintly, "I . . . I'm happy to meet you." The two odd-looking men and the vast amount of glittering, mysterious-looking equipment appeared to be getting to her.

"Well, my boy, have you made your decision?" Zacharias demanded in a businesslike fashion. "Mordecai and I have discussed the terms, and we agreed the five thousand dollars we talked about would be a fair payment for such a simple task."

Danny drew his lips together—it was now or never. "It's not as simple as you make it out to be, Uncle Zacharias. It's like jumping off a cliff on a dark night—not knowing how far down the ground is below you."

"Oh, come now!" Zacharias put out his hands palms up, his most reassuring look painted on his face. "It's not as if we're asking you to go back five thousand years and stay for a decade, Danny boy. All we want is to conduct a little *test*. You just go back a couple of hundred years, take a look around, then come back and give us a report."

"But what if something goes wrong?" Dixie piped up, a worried look on her face.

"*Wrong?*" Zacharias sounded insulted. "Nothing can go wrong, Miss Fortune! Why, I've gone over this equipment a thousand times, and I'll stake my professional reputation on it that this trip will be an unqualified success!"

Dixie shook her head stubbornly. "But it'll be Danny and me who are risking our lives, not you."

Danny's eyes popped and he yelped, "Hey—*you* aren't going with me, Dixie!"

"That's what you think!" she shot back. "And you can forget about arguing, Danny. You're not going in that thing alone—and that's all there is to it!"

Mordecai broke in before Danny could reply. "Please, let's not argue! There is no reason why the young lady can't go too—at least from a technological point of view. The Chrono-Shuttle will transport up to four people."

"And in one way it would be safer," his twin added quickly. "If for any reason you *did* have trouble, Danny— say you fainted—Dixie here could use the Recall Unit."

Suddenly it became not a question of whether Dixie was going, but *how*. "You simply can't go dressed like that, Dixie," Mordecai said disapprovingly as he studied her jeans and sweatshirt. "We have suitable clothing for Danny, but we'll have to find you something more like what girls wore three hundred years ago. That way—"

"Just a minute!" Danny interrupted loudly. "*I* have a few instructions to add before we go any further." The little men both stared at him in surprise. "Before Dixie and I climb into that thing, I want a certified check for *ten* thousand dollars made out to Mrs. Ellen Fortune. I want it in an envelope, and I want to mail it myself."

"Ten thousand dollars? Surely you're joking, young man!" Mordecai sputtered. "That's far too much money for such an easy trip."

Danny shook his head stubbornly. "You can't send Dixie without paying her! What if something happens? What about our mother?"

The two brothers leaned toward each other and whispered heatedly for a few minutes. Finally, Zacharias turned to Danny. "All right," he sighed. "We'll meet your price—but you had better make this trip worth it."

The group hopped into the great-uncles' ancient black Cadillac and headed to the bank, where Mordecai bought the certified check. Once at the post office, Danny slipped it into an envelope, sealed it, stamped it, and dropped it into the slot. "All right," he nodded. "Let's get on with it."

Finding an outfit for Dixie took more time than Danny thought it would. They made a trip to the local costume shop, where Mordecai outfitted her with a gray wool dress, practically shapeless, a knee-length wool coat, and a pair of buckle shoes so square that the right could not be told from the left. "They didn't start man-ufacturing right and left shoes until the eighteenth cen-tury," he informed her. To complete her costume, Mor-decai selected a white cotton bonnet with a starched brim in front.

The two men talked loudly as they returned to the house, but Dixie and Danny said nothing. They were sit-ting in the backseat of the big car, and Danny felt Dixie take his hand and squeeze it hard. She was trembling—probably terrified. Leaning close to her, he whispered, "It's not too late for you to change your mind."

"No!" she whispered back. She shook her head defi-antly and looked at him. "No, it's together or not at all!"

When they returned to the spooky house, they both dressed in their new clothes, Danny putting on a pair of shapeless black breeches, a worn white shirt with puffy sleeves, a wool coat, and a pair of boots as shapeless as Dixie's footwear.

"We look like gypsies!" Dixie complained.

"You won't stick out so much in these outfits," Mor-decai responded. "Now, brother, if you will give a few final instructions, we can start this little experiment."

All too soon they were back in the laboratory. "You're going back to the year 1620, the fourth day of Septem-ber—two days before the *Mayflower* sailed," Zacharias instructed. "I'll calibrate the Emerging Point to a spot about two miles outside Plymouth. All you have to do is walk into town and go to the harbor. The ship ought to be there. In any case, keep your eyes open."

"Why, you may get a glimpse of Captain Miles Stan-dish himself!" Mordecai's black eyes gleamed at the thought. "I'd love to be going myself!"

"Here—take this." Zacharias handed Danny a small

leather bag. Danny peeked in and saw a number of gold coins. "These are authentic English coins from the time you'll be visiting—just in case you need some money. We'll leave your time of return up to you, but stay at least a day. When you're ready to come back, press the button on the Recall Unit." He handed the silver disc to Danny, who took it curiously.

"I've tied it onto a leather cord so you can slip it around your neck and wear it under your shirt. That way it won't be noticeable. Just one word of warning, though," he said, and Danny looked up at him sharply. "When you press the button, be absolutely certain that you're standing together, because the next thing you know, you'll be right back in the Chrono-Shuttle! If you get separated and decide to use the device, the one who isn't within its range will be marooned in time!"

Dixie gave Danny a panicked glance.

"Well, that's it. You can climb into the machine now."

Danny slipped the cord over his head. The slim disk felt like ice against his chest. Until this moment, it had been possible to back out of this trip, but now it was too late. Danny slowly stepped into the machine and sat down in the leather-covered seat. His sister stumbled over the lip of the door and fell in beside him, her hand clutching his arm.

"Oh, by the way," Mordecai said quickly as his brother began to press keys on the control panel, "be careful not to do anything to change history. And don't be surprised if you have trouble understanding what people say, either. The English language has changed a great deal since then. The way people pronounce their vowels may sound completely different. The word *love* will sound more like *prove*, for instance." He gave his pointy beard a tug. "Maybe you ought to pretend to be from Holland or somewhere so your accents won't be as strange to them."

"A great time to bring it up!" Danny gasped. But it was too late to say anything now, for Zacharias had reached up to pull a red lever. The room was immediately filled with the same strange light and vibrations he'd seen and felt before. Only this time they were even stronger.

"Danny!" Dixie shouted, throwing her arms around him. "The light!"

An eerie green glow filled the Chrono-Shuttle and fell around them, and the entire machine began quivering at a rapid speed. Dixie hid her face against Danny's chest, but he continued to peer into the light. His great-uncles—and even the lab itself—were dissolving. With a horrible shock, he realized that he and Dixie were the ones who were dissolving. He shut his eyes tightly.

The shrill humming increased until it hurt their ears. Suddenly, the ground seemed to give way, and they were falling. *Maybe this is all a trick!* Danny panicked. *Maybe Dixie and I are really dying!*

4

AS THE GREEN LIGHT FADED, Danny thrashed around, filled with the most terrible fear he had ever known. The vibrations began to slow, and a bright light struck his eyes, causing him to close them again. A series of crashing sounds made him jump, and a nasty odor polluted the air around him.

"Dixie!" he shouted, realizing that she was no longer holding on to him.

"Right here, Danny!" He opened his eyes to see her getting to her feet and brushing the sand out of her hair. He gave her a wide-eyed stare, then relaxed. "Well, here we are in merry old England—at least I *think* so!"

They were on a sandy beach, the gray sea stretching endlessly away to the left. To the right, low sand dunes obstructed the view. Dixie moved closer to Danny, asking, "Do you really think we're in the year 1620?"

He shrugged. "I don't know. But look down the beach. . . ." She followed his gesture, and he added, "That looks like a town, doesn't it? No big buildings, but I doubt we'll find any skyscrapers if this really *is* 1620." He shivered. "Come on, Dix! It's *cold* out here!"

They began to walk along the beach, wondering what to expect. It was a chilly day, even though the sun was high in the sky. After they had walked half an hour, they began to notice shacks set back off the shore and small fishing boats far out at sea. Finally the beach swept to their left. "Look, Dixie—this is the harbor. See all the ships?"

"It's cute, isn't it?" Dixie said. The harbor was packed with boats of all sizes and types. Some of them were huge ships of war, some were obviously transport ships, heavily loaded. Hundreds of small fishing boats scurried across the harbor like water bugs.

Danny led the way down the beach to where a small boat was pulled up onto the sand. They saw a single dinghy, its white sail covered with patches. Two men on the beach were hanging nets on some sort of a frame. When they got close enough, Danny called out, "Hello!"

"Hullo, yerself!" the older of the two men replied. They wore well-used clothing and their hands were rough and red with the cold. "Where be ye a'goin, yonkers?"

Though the man's speech was thick and sounded strange, Danny had no trouble understanding him. "Just out walking," Danny answered, his relief showing in his voice. "Is this Plymouth?"

"Aye, it be that," the other man said. He eyed at the two suspiciously and asked again, "Where be ye goin'?"

"We're looking for a ship—the *Mayflower*. Have you heard of it?"

"Certainly." The sailor nodded. He took a clay pipe out of his mouth and pointed with it. "There she lies. Captain Christopher Jones in command."

"Be ye goin' to join the other loonies?" the other man piped up, bursting into loud laughter. He nodded wisely and tapped his forehead. "Right out of Bedlam, they be—all of 'em!"

The older man shook his head and, frowning at the

speaker, said sharply, "Never ye mind that, Rob!" Then he pursed his lips and added, "A bit of bad luck, it was, about the *Speedwell*, but naught to be done about it."

"The *Speedwell*?" Danny asked, looking out toward the harbor.

"Ye ain't heard about that?" the older man asked in surprise. "Why, them folks has had a hard time! Some of 'em set out from Holland—Leyden it was—in that smaller craft yon, and met up with the *Mayflower* at Plymouth. Then both craft set sail fer the New World back in August—"

"And both of 'em come limpin' back a week ago!" the younger man snorted. "And now it's goin' about that Cap'n Jones is a'goin' to stuff *all* of 'em onto his own boat and carry 'em over!" He spat on the sand and shook his head, adding moodily, "If God had wanted people to get across the water, He wouldn't have let the *Speedwell* spring her stays so they had to come back to port!"

Danny suddenly couldn't wait to see the famous *Mayflower*. "Thank you for the information." He nodded his head politely and began to lead Dixie away. "Boy, it's lucky they came back, or we'd have missed seeing the *Mayflower*! Or would we have?" He scratched his head. "It's hard to understand how this traveling back in time thing works." As they made their way along the harbor, he added, "I never knew there were two ships that started out, did you?"

"No," Dixie admitted, then laughed. "We should have brought a history book along, I guess!" Her face suddenly grew serious. "Danny, you've still got the Recall Unit, right?"

"Better believe it!" he grinned. "Right here." He pulled open his wool coat to expose the unit dangling in its worn leather pouch from a leather cord. Mordecai had insisted it would attract less attention if it were hidden. Danny tapped it confidently. "*Nothing* is going to get this little hummer off me! It's our passport back home."

They walked slowly along the beach, fascinated by the sights. Soon they approached a long dock built of pilings. "I think that's it," Danny said, pointing to a ship that was anchored about two hundred yards out. "Doesn't look very big, does it?"

"No, it sure doesn't," she answered. "I wish we could go on board to explore. Wouldn't that be something to tell Mordecai about!" She shaded her eyes and shouted, "Look, Danny! A little boat is coming in—maybe we'll see some real Pilgrims!"

They watched eagerly as the small boat propelled by three sets of oars bobbed up and down on the low swells. It came right to the dock where they stood, and a man dressed in plain gray clothing climbed out, accompanied by two boys about the twins' age, as well as a pair of girls not much older. Another man got out, this one sunburned and dressed in a more colorful costume. "Mr. Bradford," the man said. "We'll have to sail at once—tomorrow or the day after at most."

"Dixie," Danny whispered, "that's *William Bradford*! He's the leader of the Pilgrims."

The twins stared at him. It was weird to actually see someone step right out of a history book. "I agree, Captain Jones," Bradford was saying. "Let me talk to our people. Some will have to stay here now that the *Mayflower* is our only craft. Walk with me to the inn and we'll discuss it." Then he added, "We're having a service, but you may speak to the people before it begins."

As the two walked away, a voice near them said, "What's your name, lass?" Danny spun around to see that one of the boys had come to stand beside Dixie. He was probably about fifteen and was tall and muscular with blond hair and brown eyes.

"It's Dixie," she answered without thinking.

"Dixie? Never heard of a lass named that!" He laughed and said, "I'm John Billington—and that's my brother, Francis."

"I'm glad to meet you. This is my brother Danny."

"You talk funny," John said, regarding her. "You'll not be from these parts, I'm thinking." He glanced at Danny and then back to Dixie. "Like two peas, aren't they, Francis?"

The other boy came forward. Francis was clearly a couple of years younger and not so strong looking. He smiled shyly and nodded. "Be you going on a ship like us?"

"I'd like to very much," Dixie said. "But we've just been on a long journey."

The two girls came closer, both of them wearing dark heavy coats. One had black hair and deep brown eyes; the other was also dark and not as tall. "We'll be having a service tonight," the taller girl said. She gave Danny a careful look, as if measuring him up, before giving him a smile. "If you'd like to come, you'd be welcome. I'm Constance Hopkins," she added smoothly, "and this is Elizabeth Tilley."

Danny gave Dixie a quick look to see what she thought of the idea. "We'd like to come to the service—if we wouldn't be butting in."

"Butting in?" Constance asked. "What does that mean?"

"Oh, just that we don't want to . . . to intrude," Danny stumbled, aware that language was going to be somewhat of a problem after all.

Constance laughed. "Everyone is welcome. Come along with us." Before Danny knew what was happening, she had a firm grip on his arm.

Why, who would have guessed that a Pilgrim girl would be such a flirt! Danny was shocked to realize that the girls of the *Mayflower* company were probably not much different from the girls of his own time. And Pilgrims had always seemed so stuffy!

The trip through the town was exciting. It was odd to see such short buildings—none were over three stories, and most of them were only one. Even though smoke rose from chimneys, the air seemed clear—there were no cars to send clouds of carbon monoxide into the atmosphere. Danny took a deep breath, expecting to enjoy his first breath of absolutely pure air. He almost gagged!

"What in the world is that *horrible* smell?" he choked.

"Smell?" Constance asked. She sniffed the air and turned to him, curiosity written on her face. "I don't smell anything."

Neither did anyone else, apparently—except for Dixie. "I think it's coming from the ditch over there, Danny." She pointed to a shallow ditch full of sludge and food scraps that ran down the center of the cobblestone street. "It's the sewer, I think."

"Oh yes!" John said proudly. "Isn't it wonderful! All the garbage and slop used to lay in the street, but now that the city's put that drain in, the rain washes it away in no time. See?" Even as he spoke a woman threw a waterfall of terrible-smelling slop from her upstairs window onto the cobblestones close by. It splashed every-where. John laughed and smiled proudly. "It's a wonderful invention. What will people think of next!"

Danny wrinkled his nose. For the first time in his life he realized what a luxury a modern sewage system was. But the world of Plymouth was too busy for him to spend much time thinking about garbage. Carts and coaches rumbled down the street at speeds Danny had never imagined people could get out of horse-drawn ve-hicles. At every corner they encountered men, women, and children—some in the sooty rags of chimney sweeps, others dressed in the rich satin and gold of the aristocracy. Some were gazing out at the pedestrians from chairs carried by men with thick legs. Porters sweated in the cold air under their burdens, and trades-men scurried around like ants.

Finally they passed through a number of curving, crooked streets, which totally confused Danny. This sec-tion of Plymouth was much quieter. "What's the name of this street, Elizabeth?" he asked. She had moved closer to take the arm not held by Constance.

The pretty girl stared at him. "Name? Why would anyone name a street?" she asked in wonder.

"Well, what about numbers? Are the buildings num-bered?" Elizabeth gave him a funny look and shook her head.

"But how do you find anything?" he asked.

Constance pulled at his arm to distract his attention from Elizabeth. "What a silly question! If you want to know where something is—say maybe the Eagle Inn—all you have to do is ask and someone will tell you, 'Why, it's just down the street from the old Town Meeting Hall.' " Danny could tell it had never occurred to her that some people might not have heard of *that*, either!

They arrived shortly at a two-story building built of stone. It was covered with peeling white plaster, and heavy timbers held up the structure. A faded sign with a crude painting of a bird that looked more like a buzzard than an eagle hung over the door. Danny assumed this was the inn they were talking about. William Bradford turned and noticed them for the first time. His eyes searched them carefully, and he asked, "Are these your friends, Master Billington?"

"Yes, sir. This is Danny and Dixie . . . Fortune," he added with prompting from Dixie. "We've invited them to the meeting—with your permission."

Bradford studied young Billington. "You're welcome to bring them. I've been hoping that some of you would join us." He nodded and smiled at the twins. "I must warn you that we have some business to take care of— so we may have to cut the service short." He shook his head. "I doubt we'll have more than four or five hours for the service—and I do hate to pare a sermon down to less than two hours!"

Dixie mouthed the words "A two-hour sermon!" with her lips, but Danny shook his head at her in warning. "Thank you for asking us, sir."

Once inside, they were introduced to Captain Christopher Jones, a short but powerful-looking man with a booming voice. He moved to the front of the room and insisted that the group sail at once. "You will be getting to the New World very late in the year as it is—too late, I think. You'll have to build shelter and gather food before the worst of winter comes." He paused dramatically. "I don't know that it can be done."

"Thank you, Captain," Elder Bradford said courteously when the captain had finished. "We will all be aboard by day after tomorrow. As for the danger—God will see us through."

The actual service began as soon as the captain left. Dixie and Danny had attended church quite regularly, but they were taken off guard by several things. "Look at the bright colors they're wearing, Danny," Dixie whispered. "Especially the women. I thought Pilgrims always wore black!"

The twins were also surprised to find that the people did not sit with their families. The men took their seats on hard wooden benches on one side, while the women sat across the aisle. The children were placed under the stern and watchful eyes of the deacons.

Everyone stood up to pray. By the time they finished almost an hour later, Danny was ready to fall over. "Don't these people ever stop?" he murmured to his sister.

"Shh," Dixie whispered. "Something's going to happen." A small, pale-faced man dressed in black clothing and black gloves got up. He read aloud from a huge Bible, pausing often to comment, and then they sang a psalm. There were no instruments and the tune was sung from memory.

Danny was usually bored with church, but there was something about the way these people sang that interested him. They all seemed to enjoy it so much. He looked around the room—almost every face was lit up with happiness. He caught Dixie's eye and realized that she was sensing the same thing.

After an hour of singing, the man dressed in black stood up to preach the sermon. It lasted for at least an hour, but Danny was surprised to discover that he almost enjoyed it. *I nearly die when I have to listen to a*

twenty-minute sermon at home, but this one is different.
He really has something to say.

At last the service ended. Before he could move,
Danny found Constance Hopkins and Elizabeth Tilley
surrounding him like a pair of bookends. "Let's go have
something to eat, everyone," Constance invited, and
they all moved to the back of the room.

"I'll get you some food, Dixie," John said, turning to
a long, low table set with round loaves of fresh bread,
butter, cold cuts of meat, and large containers of fresh
milk. For dessert, there were some juicy tarts and
sweets.

"That was a great service," Danny said, reaching for
another slice of meat. "I enjoyed it."

"Did you now?" John had returned and was looking
at him with some surprise. He shrugged. "I was bored
to death."

"But don't you go to church all the time?"

"Church! Not likely!" The idea seemed to amuse
John. He bit into a slice of fresh bread plastered with
butter, then waved it as he answered. "These are the
Saints," he explained. "They're all religious folks—fanatics if you listen to what people say. They left England
'bout eleven years ago to go live in Holland and worship
God the way they wanted. But now the Spanish are
threatening Holland, so they're on their way to the New
World."

"But what about you?" Dixie asked.

John laughed shortly, "The Saints couldn't get
enough folks to make the trip. We joined up with them."
A irritated look crossed his forehead, and he added,
"They call us Strangers."

"Saints and Strangers?" Dixie was surprised. "If

you're a Stranger, why are you here at church with the Saints?"

John squeezed her arm and smiled. "When you walked up, I decided to come to church to be with the prettiest lass in Plymouth."

Dixie blushed and looked confused. Danny knew that she'd never had a boy pay her so much attention.

"Well, church is over now," Danny stated. He didn't like the way John was looking at his sister.

"Oh, it isn't over yet!" John informed him. "There'll be more preaching after a while." He paused. "You know, we'll be leaving day after tomorrow."

Constance broke into the conversation. "I wish *you* were coming with us, Danny and Dixie. It'd make the trip sweeter!"

"So do I," Dixie said.

John looked at her with interest. "Where are you going, anyway?"

"Oh, we . . . we don't have any particular plans," she faltered.

"Do you have work—or a family here in Plymouth?" When she shook her head, he looked at Danny and said, "Say, I have a proposition for you."

"What's that?" Danny asked.

"There's a need for some indentured servants with our group. Dr. Samuel Fuller would take you two on right now!"

Danny smiled and gave Dixie a quick glance. "That's kind of you to think of it, John, but—"

"Don't be offended," John said quickly. "But do you have any money for a place to stay, or food?"

"Well, to tell you the truth—" Danny began but was cut off.

"I thought as much." John looked at the pair and lowered his voice. "You can stay with me tonight, Danny, and Constance and Elizabeth can look out for Dixie." He laughed and said, "You two lasses try to convince Dixie to board the *Mayflower*, and I'll do the same for Danny here. It'd be good to have you with us."

Constance and Elizabeth giggled, and suddenly Danny wanted to stay a little longer. "Dixie—it's getting late. Do you want to go home"—as he said the word, he patted the Recall Unit so she would understand his meaning—"or do you want to stay the night?"

Dixie looked at him intently. "Oh, let's at least stay until tomorrow!"

"Can't say no to that, can you, Danny?" John grinned. "Now first thing tomorrow we'll take both of you onto the ship." He slapped Danny on the shoulder and smiled. "The two of you don't look like the kind who'd say no to an adventure like this—sailing across the ocean to a New World!"

Danny smiled at Dixie—if only John knew the truth! "We've made at least one long and adventurous trip, John. And I'd sure like to see the ship." To himself, Danny added, *After all, what harm can it do to look?*

5

DANNY FORTUNE HAD NEVER SPENT a more uncomfortable night. He shared a rough blanket with the
Billington brothers in a tiny room above a tavern. There
had been at least ten or twelve other men and boys trying to sleep on the hard floor. If the rowdy singing and
shouting filtering up from the tavern below had not kept
him awake, the rumbling snores from his sleeping
neighbors would have done the job. As if that were not
enough, his feet began to itch fiercely—by midnight he
was clawing at his entire body. Danny had become a
home for fleas!

He rose at dawn looking more tired than he had felt
the night before. None of the others seemed the least bit
affected. John and Francis led Danny outside to a pump,
where he washed his face in cold water. After that, they
went inside the tavern for a breakfast of cold meat and
hard rolls. Danny found himself missing his usual bowl
of cold cereal.

John Billington Sr. joined them. He was a large red-
faced man with close-set black eyes. He listened as his
son introduced Danny, then nodded shortly. "Aye, Fuller
does want a couple of servants—if he's not already
signed some."

"He's not done that," his wife Sarah sniffed. She reluctantly put a small portion of the cold meat in front of

Danny, adding sharply, "If you plan on signing papers of indenture with Fuller, you'd best go eat with him."

She was so rude, Danny almost shoved the food back at her, but he was too hungry. He ate quickly, picking up the names of those around the table as he did. Constance Hopkins smiled and waved at him, and he identified the middle-aged, balding man near her as her father Stephen Hopkins and the small woman beside him as her mother, Elizabeth. Constance came over as he finished, whispering, "Come on, Danny. Let's go down to the wharf."

He got up and followed her, and the two of them walked along streets that were already busy with tradesmen. The air was cold, and when Constance saw him shiver, she shook her head in sympathy. "You need a heavier coat, Danny. Maybe I can find one of my brother's to fit you—but then you're so big and tall I don't think you could wear it." She looked up at him with a quick smile.

"Why . . . that would be nice," Danny gulped, then blushed. Besides Dixie, he had never been comfortable talking with girls, and Constance was so pretty that he was doubly nervous around her.

"Have you decided to go?" she asked.

"Well, I'll have to talk to my sister." That wasn't what he had intended to say, but it just popped out. He shrugged his shoulders. "Running off on the *Mayflower* isn't exactly something a person should do without thinking." *Especially when that person doesn't belong here in the first place,* he added silently.

Constance became quiet, but he knew she had not given up on the idea. He was glad when they arrived at the wharf. They made it just in time to squeeze into the small boat with Dixie, Elizabeth Tilley, and several other people. It was propelled by six sailors who sent the small craft swiftly across the harbor. In a short time, they were alongside the ship.

Danny and Dixie scrambled up the side of the vessel eagerly. The deck was swarming with people. Sailors cursed everyone who got in their way. Children, underfoot and in constant danger of being stepped on, scurried everywhere, and men and women passengers carried bags and boxes down into the lower part of the ship.

"It's so *crowded*!" Dixie exclaimed. A husky, good-looking man of about twenty paused to look at her.

"Crowded? Why, not *half* the passengers are on board!" He looked more carefully at the newcomers. "Be you the indentured servants?"

"Not yet," Constance piped up and gave the man a dazzling smile. Danny suddenly realized that Constance Hopkins could no more help flirting than she could help breathing. The thought took the wind out of his sails—he had already begun to think quite a lot of himself since meeting Constance.

"This is Danny and Dixie Fortune," she said, "and this is John Alden. He's our cooper." Danny looked puzzled, and she laughed. "He makes barrels," she explained. She put her hand on Alden's arm and added, "He's a *very* important part of the company because all our water is in barrels—and he has to see that they don't leak."

John Alden smiled at her, then looked across the deck. "There's Dr. Fuller." He pointed toward a large, thick-bodied man with a black beard and a pock-marked face. "He's the man needing some servants. Come along and I'll introduce you."

"Hello," said Samuel Fuller as Alden and the group strode up. He listened to Alden describe the twins' situation for a moment, then gave the pair a close inspection. "Let's see your hands," he demanded. When Danny hesitated, he reached out and grabbed them. Running his own hard palm over Danny's, he snorted. "Why, this hand's not done any work!" Then he did the same for Dixie and shook his head, saying, "I need workers, not aristocrats!"

"We're not looking for a job," Danny said, resenting the way this man was treating them. Just who did he think he was? "Mr. Alden made a mistake." His face was slightly red with embarrassment. "We just want to see the ship before she sails."

"Better look quickly, then," John Alden said cheerfully. "Tomorrow we'll be on the high seas!" Then he added, "Best to stay out of the sailors' way, though. They're a rough crew."

"John," Constance pouted, "why don't *you* show us around? None of the sailors would dare insult us while you are with us!"

Alden laughed and grinned at them. "All right. Come on." He ushered them along the deck. "She's a sweet ship," he said fondly. "She's carried wine and cognac from France, so she doesn't stink like most. She's one hundred and thirteen feet from stern to bowsprit. There's a gun deck about twenty-six feet wide and seventy-eight feet long between the hold and the upper deck—that's where most of the passengers will stay."

Many families were already settling in as they made their way through the narrow space. They reminded Danny of birds building a nest as they arranged their few things just so. Every inch of the ship would have to be used.

Alden led them on to the crew's quarters. A large area of the sleeping compartment was taken up by the galley, not leaving much space for the thirty men who used it.

"How do they all fit?" Dixie asked.

Alden smiled. "Only half the men are ever in it at one time—the rest are on duty."

By the time they had seen the captain's cabin and the rest of the ship, the fresh air above deck was a welcome change to Danny. The odors created by so many people living so close together were already strong. But the experience of being on the *Mayflower* was so exciting that they spent all afternoon roaming the ship, storing up information to report to their great-uncles.

"We'll never get another chance like this, Dixie!" Danny commented as they stood on deck watching the group of Pilgrim leaders who were having a conference beside the rail.

"I'm going to find Elizabeth Tilley," Dixie announced suddenly. "I'll be back in a little while."

"Okay," Danny nodded. "I'll just keep exploring the ship."

Dixie left, and Danny entertained himself by listening in on other people's conversations. Eventually, his sleepless night caught up with him, and he sat down to rest below deck. When he leaned his head back, a small boy came up to introduce himself. "My name is Resolved."

Danny opened his eyes and saw a round-eyed boy of six or so standing beside him. "Hi," he said.

Resolved looked up at the overhead timbers. "What's high?"

Danny laughed—he kept forgetting to think before talking. Danny lay back against a sack of grain that was wedged behind him. *It sure is strange to know that I'm really on board the* Mayflower, he thought before drifting off.

Danny woke with a start and looked around wildly. It took him a moment to remember where he was. Scrambling to his feet, he raced to find Dixie, who was on deck talking with John and Francis Billington.

"Well, lass," John was saying, "I hope Constance has persuaded you to come along."

"Actually, I think she's spent most of her time trying to persuade *Danny* to go," Dixie said innocently. Danny wanted to laugh.

Constance simply giggled and nodded. "We need some lively young people," she said. "Too many dry, dusty preachers on this ship to suit me!"

Their group walked around, getting in the way of those on deck with work to do. When Danny finally managed to get Dixie alone for a few moments, he said, "Boy, this is really incredible, isn't it? I wish I had a camera!"

Dixie glanced around them and said softly, "I never thought about the Pilgrims being real people, did you, Danny? I mean, they're just like everybody else."

"Well, not *quite*," Danny said slowly. He looked at the ship swarming with people and shook his head. "They've given up everything they have to go on this voyage. And just look at the size of this ship! It's much smaller than I thought it would be."

"I know," Dixie agreed. "And to think the Saints are

doing it all just to be able to worship God the way they want to. Uncle Mordecai sure was wrong about them." She looked a little ashamed as she continued, "I guess I've learned one thing here—I don't take God seriously enough. He probably wasn't too thrilled with me. Just look at the way I acted the other day!"

"Me either," Danny said thoughtfully. He looked out across the harbor at the gray sea. "Think what it would mean if we *had* to cross that big ocean, Dixie. I don't think I could cut it."

"Well," she said quickly, "at least we don't have to go—and I'm glad, too, because it would scare me to death." She brushed a stray hair back from her face. "By the way, when *are* we going to go back home?"

"There's no rush, Dixie, if you don't mind. Mordecai will want a full report. If we hang around one more night and see them off tomorrow, we'll have quite the story." He made a face. "I guess I can stand one more night of being eaten alive by bedbugs!"

Dixie shook her head. "Danny, I don't *want* to stay." Her face looked strained. "This time-travel thing scares me—it really does! It's so . . . so *weird*! I didn't sleep at all last night. I kept thinking, 'What if the Recall Unit doesn't work?' I want to go home now!"

Her eyes were filling with tears, and Danny felt guilty for pushing her. "Please don't cry, Dixie! It's no big deal. We'll slip away on the next boat. As soon as we're out of sight, we'll use the Recall Unit. Okay?"

"Thanks!" she said gratefully, a smile returning to her face. "I know you'd like to stay longer, but—"

"We've already stayed a day. We've seen enough," he reassured her. Then he turned his head and spotted some activity off to their right. "Look! They're taking the boat back for another load. This is our chance!" The two of them climbed into the boat. Danny was relieved not to be spotted by Constance or John.

When the boat reached the shore, they walked the wharf, taking a final look at the famous ship. Then they ducked behind some fishing nets hanging out to dry.

"This is a good spot," Danny said. "We can go back to our time while taking our last look at the *Mayflower*."

They watched the ship rising and falling in the water for a few minutes, then Danny reached inside his shirt to retrieve the Recall Unit.

It wasn't there!

Dixie turned to look at him, and her face paled. "What's the matter?"

Danny opened his mouth to speak, but his mouth was so dry nothing came out. He felt sick to his stomach.

"Danny! What is it?" She took his arm. "Are you sick?"

"The . . . the Recall Unit! It's *gone!*"

Dixie's eyes grew large. "No! It *can't* be!"

He yanked his shirt out of his pants and stared down the neck of his shirt at his bare chest. "It's really gone!" he groaned. "Oh, great—now what will we do?"

"Maybe the cord broke," Dixie suggested hopefully. "Let's go back the way we came. Maybe we'll find it on the beach."

"There's no way!" he moaned. "That cord was too strong to break by itself. Wait a minute—let me think. . . . I had it on when we went on the ship. I know that much because I checked it as we boarded. But wait—"

"What is it?"

"I . . . I went to sleep down below deck for a little

while. Not for long," he said defensively. "Just for twenty minutes or so."

She stared at him in horror. "You don't think someone would *steal* it, do you? Why would a Pilgrim—"

"That has to be it!" he interrupted her. "There's no way it could have fallen off."

"But how would anyone get it off without waking you up?"

"Why, someone could just slice the cord with a sharp knife and slip it off," Danny said. "And I'm sure there are plenty of folks on that ship who'd steal if they got a chance!"

"But not the Pilgrims?"

"Maybe not the Saints, but we've already found out that some of the Pilgrims aren't Christians at all. It could have been a Stranger. And besides, the sailors are all over the ship. Any one of them could have come by, seen that cord, and taken the Recall Unit."

They stood there a moment, the silence of the beach broken only by the seagulls and the slapping sound the waves made as they patted the sand at the twins' feet. Across the harbor, the *Mayflower* rose and fell, and they could see the passengers and crew moving over the deck.

Danny could tell by the look on Dixie's face that she was petrified with fear. He had already thought of the terrible possibility that the Recall Unit might not work at all—but now that it was missing, he was so frightened he could not even think.

Dixie began to cry, and Danny clumsily put an arm around her shoulder—wishing that he'd never even seen the Chrono-Shuttle.

It's up to me. I'm the one who got us into this mess,

he told himself. His mind felt paralyzed. Desperate, he tried to think of some solution—something to do, some way to get out of the horrible trap they were in—but he knew there was no escape without the Recall Unit.

Finally he cleared his throat and said as bravely as he could, "Dixie, I know you're scared, but let's not blow this thing out of proportion—"

"Out of proportion!" she wailed. "We're stuck forever in the year 1620—never going to see our family again! And you say I'm—you've got a lot of nerve!"

Her voice was becoming hysterical. Afraid of attracting attention, he quickly covered her mouth with his hand. "I've got a plan. All we have to do," he said slowly, "is get on the ship. Sooner or later we'll find the person who took the unit. And as soon as we do, we'll be right back in the Chrono-Shuttle!"

Dixie stopped crying, but she could not control her sniffles. "Do you *really* think so?" she whispered, looking up at him.

"Sure!" Danny nodded with a great deal more confidence than he felt.

"If you say so," Dixie whispered.

He swallowed hard. "Well, I know what we have to do next. We need to get Dr. Fuller to take us on as his servants. It'll be hard, but we don't have much choice."

The twins walked quickly back down the beach and waited at the wharf until the small boat was ready to go back to the *Mayflower*. "Can we ride back with you?" Danny asked the mate. The man agreed.

They were the only passengers—the small craft was piled high with supplies. "Is this the lot, Clarke?" one of the sailors asked.

The tall man in charge nodded. "At last! We'll catch

the tide early tomorrow—and about time, too." He spat over the side and shook his head with contempt, adding, "These fools will get to the New World with the dead of winter facing them. Should have left three months ago!"

"Aye!" the sailor nodded as he stroked his oar. "It's tempting the Lord, they are!"

"Don't know about that," Clarke shrugged. "But they don't have good sense. I reckon most of them will be dead in six months, either butchered by the savages or starved!"

The conversation did little to cheer their passengers, but Danny squeezed Dixie's arm to reassure her. "We know they'll make it, though—don't we, Dixie?" he whispered. "After all, it's the *Mayflower*!"

As soon as the boat was secured, they went on deck. "There's the doctor. Come on, Dixie." Danny led her up to Dr. Fuller, who was standing by himself gazing out over the water.

"Dr. Fuller?" Danny began nervously, and when the big man turned to look at him, he cleared his throat. "I— that is *we* . . . we were wondering if . . ."

Fuller stared down at the pair, seemingly annoyed at having his thoughts interrupted. "Well, what is it, boy?" he asked gruffly.

"Well, the thing is—Dixie and I, we need a place to go," Danny began again. Then, seeing the man's heavy face begin to cloud, he added, "I know we're not exactly what you're looking for, but we'll work hard!"

Fuller shook his head, his dark eyes thoughtful. "I'm in need of servants, but you're too soft. I don't know what you've been doing, but neither of you is tough enough to stand what we're going to run into." He waved his thick hand at the passengers milling around. "Why, this is a pretty tough young bunch, but even *they* don't have any idea of what's waiting. Nor do I, for that matter."

"Dr. Fuller, we don't have anyone else to ask," Dixie pleaded. "Please let us go. We may be soft, but we can learn!"

Fuller picked up her hand. Examining it, he remarked quietly, "Lass, this hand would be raw with blisters. There's wood to cut, houses to build, and nothing to start with! We'll be set ashore with nothing but a few crude tools, and the land will kill us if we fail!"

Danny nodded his understanding, but kept insisting, "I promise you, sir, that we'll work hard for you—we'll give you our best."

Fuller looked Danny right in the eye as if searching to find out what he was made of. Finally he shrugged his burly shoulders. "All right, then, it's a bargain. You'll be bound to me for seven years, and after that you're free. I'll feed you and clothe you. Come with me now, and we'll have Mr. Bradford draw up the indentures." As he led them along the deck, he paused once and said, "You realize, don't you, that we're all in God's hands? He's all we have to trust in right now."

Danny looked out over the vast ocean before answering. God had never seemed very important to him in his own time. "Yes, sir. Dixie and I know that."

Dixie nodded and gripped Danny's hand tightly. He could tell her fear was still there, but she seemed calmer than she had been on the beach. Maybe, just maybe, things would be okay.

6

DIXIE AND DANNY, stiff with the morning chill, gathered with the other passengers on deck as the sun's gray light broke on September 6, 1620. Everyone stood back respectfully as Captain Christopher Jones, dressed in his best cloth doublet and a clean white shirt, his curly black hair plastered close to his head, popped out of the hatch onto the deck. For one moment he stood completely still, then suddenly he put his hands to his mouth and shouted into the still morning air.

"Mr. Clarke! Weigh anchor! We'll wait no longer!"

The sailors began to unfurl the sails, and a sudden gust filled out the mainsail with a loud crack. The excitement over, most of the passengers went below, but Dixie and Danny stayed on deck. The *Mayflower's* blunt cutwater rose and fell as the ship plowed through the dark frills of water. The effort made the boat creak and strain so loudly it sounded alive.

Danny moved to the stern for one last look at England. He found himself standing close enough to hear what William Bradford was saying to Dr. Samuel Fuller and Edward Winslow. "Think of it, brethren—no one in England is giving us a passing thought as we begin our voyage." Bradford's eyes were fixed on the disappearing shore.

"In London they're talking about the king's weakness

in dealing with Spain," he continued thoughtfully. "Spain has joined the war, and the English court is in an uproar over it. Holland may well be attacked soon. All Europe seems ready to go up in flames."

He paused and looked over the deck with a faint smile, then added softly, "And here we are—a handful of tattered exiles sailing west in a weather-beaten freighter, believing that God is sending us to start a new world. Most people say we're deluded."

Bradford hesitated for a moment, and Edward Winslow said quickly, "Aye, that's so, Mr. Bradford—but most have been wrong before!"

Fuller nodded, the wind ruffling his mass of black hair. "Never fear, sir, we'll have our place in history." He glanced at Dixie's pale, tense face, and his expression grew serious. "It won't come easy, though—nothing worthwhile ever does!"

His words proved true. The mild breezes that drove the *Mayflower* out of the harbor lasted for only a few days. Many of the passengers grew seasick—Danny and Dixie among them. Packed as they were on board the small ship, the misery of the voyage hit at once. There was no heat except in the galley, and the North Atlantic was always cold. There was no chance to wash except in saltwater and no plumbing, either—only buckets. People never undressed, but wore the same outfit every day—if their clothes accidentally got wet, they stayed wet until the sun came out to dry them. No mattresses or blankets were provided, and as for privacy—that could only be found in the cabin of Captain Christopher Jones!

Once Dixie and Danny's stomachs settled, there was the problem of getting used to the food. The only meat was pickled in a salty brine to preserve it. Saucer-sized wheat and dried pea flour biscuits were also on the menu, along with Holland cheese, mush, oatmeal, and pease pudding—a thick, unappetizing pudding made from peas and eggs. There was almost no chance to eat a hot meal; the galley was barred to non-crew members. And with only one cook to feed the thirty-man crew, it was impossible to feed a hundred passengers!

Danny and Dixie were thoroughly sick of the food by the end of the first week. One day they were treated to a small serving of plum duff, a pudding made of beef suet and a few raisins and prunes. As they gobbled it down— it didn't taste as bad as Danny thought it would—Dixie licked her fingers. "Oh, what I wouldn't give for one good Snickers!"

John Billington gave her a surprised look. "A *snicker*? Why, go on and have one, then. No law against laughing, I reckon."

"No, I mean a candy bar," she sighed. "And I'd give a year of my life for one hot dog!"

Constance was sitting with their little group, and she stared at Dixie in amazement. "A *hot dog*? Why in the world would you want a hot *dog*?"

Danny gave Dixie a warning look. "Oh, that's what we used to call special kind of meat back home—a hot dog. It gets boring eating all this cold food, don't you think?"

John took a spoonful of his lobscouse, a thick soup filled with chunks of salt meat, then held up his biscuit. "Better enjoy the food now," he commented. "The sailors say that by the time we've been to sea for a couple of weeks, we'll have to tap the biscuits on the table before we eat them."

"What for?" Dixie asked.

"To knock out the weevils and the little brown grubs." He grinned, then laughed as Dixie turned a pasty white. "You've been brought up too easy, lass," he noted. "But you'll learn to work soon enough when we get to the New World."

Dixie changed the subject. "How's your mother, Constance?"

"Oh, fine. It looks like the baby will be born before we land, though." She put her arm loosely through Danny's. He squirmed.

"Are you glad you came?" John asked.

"Well, it's been interesting so far, but it's not like I thought it would be," Danny admitted. "I mean, I thought everybody on the *Mayflower* would be just one big happy family—but it's more like a little war."

"That's so," John agreed. "The thirty Saints all seem to get along with each other well enough. But they sure don't seem to like us Strangers. There are a lot more of us than there are of them, but the Saints act as if they want to rule us all."

"I think you're right about that," Danny nodded. "But you're forgetting the hired men like John Alden and the indentured servants like Dixie and me. It's hard for us to know who to side with sometimes."

"I think there'll be trouble soon enough," Constance said. "And the crew—what about them? They're awful! I never heard such language." She got to her feet and pulled at Danny to join her. "Come on, let's go to the rear of the ship and watch the wake."

He followed her, and for the next hour they stood watching the wild white water stirred up by the ship as it pushed through the gray sea. Constance was a ready talker, so Danny had only to nod and say "uh-huh" from time to time to keep his end of the conversation going. He was tired—it was impossible to sleep in the tiny corner he shared with dozens of others. Ship life was worse than he'd ever imagined it would be, giving him and Dixie added incentive to find the Recall Unit. But after two weeks of searching, they still hadn't found a clue.

A loud voice interrupted his thoughts. "Well, now, ain't this sweet! Two little lovebirds!" A stocky sailor stood leering down at them. He moved toward Constance and said, "Why, a sweet little thing like you don't need no plucked chicken like this 'un!" As Constance rose to her feet, he caught her arm. The girl looked disgusted and tried to pull away.

Danny, angry at the sailor for latching on to his friend, gathered up his courage and demanded, "Let her go and get out of here!"

"Tell you what," the sailor replied, his eyes burning, "Why don't *you* go away. That way, the lady and me can 'ave a talk."

Without thinking, Danny stepped forward and yanked hard at the burly sailor's arm. A second later, he found himself on the deck with his head spinning. The masts were going around in circles! When they stopped, he got to his feet and saw that John Alden had appeared and was standing between the sailor and Constance.

"I'll bust your head!" The sailor reached out for Alden and found himself caught in a pair of steely arms. He struggled to break free, but Alden gave a twist and sent the man wheeling through the air. He hit the deck with a loud *thump*, but was up in an instant, cursing violently and reaching inside his jacket as he started toward Alden.

"That'll be enough, Salterne!" They all turned to see

that Captain Jones had appeared, apparently coming from the poop deck. His gray eyes were snapping. "Get about your work, Salterne—and if you trouble the passengers again, you'll find yourself needing a new back. I'll take the one you have off with a cane!"

The sailor swallowed and left, shooting Alden a look of hatred. "He's an evil-tongued fellow," Captain Jones said. "Like the rest of them. Are you all right, young man? What's your name?"

"Danny Fortune, sir! And I'm not hurt." The full force of what he had tried to do was just hitting Danny. *I've got to be more careful—I can't get myself killed. What would Dixie do if I died here in the past?*

"Good." Captain Jones turned to the husky young cooper and said, "You've made yourself an enemy, Alden. I wouldn't wander about deck after dark if I were you."

John Alden shrugged carelessly. "I'll not lose sleep over that one, Captain."

"If you like a fight, you'd better get to the main deck," Captain Jones smiled. "I think Captain Standish is about to begin his lesson on military procedures."

Alden hurried away, and Constance pulled at Danny. "Come on, let's see what they're up to!"

They hurried to the main deck to find white-haired Carver, who'd been chosen as governor, making a speech. He stood very straight, making him seem taller than he was. "We must be prepared to defend ourselves as soon as we land," he said in a clear voice. "And we are blessed to have Captain Miles Standish as our military advisor. He has served the king in many military actions."

"I don't need no tin soldier to teach me how to fight!"

John Billington Sr. snapped sullenly.

"You will learn with the rest, sir!" Carver silenced him.

Danny watched with interest as Standish stepped forward—he was one of the most famous of all the Pilgrims. "I like the way he looks!" Danny whispered to Dixie, who had also come to see the training. Standish was a small, tough-looking man wearing seasoned leather breeches and a belted leather-lined jacket. A burnished steel helmet decorated with a crimson band sat on his red hair, and he had a shrill voice.

"You will all learn to use this weapon," he said, holding up a musket. "This is a matchlock. It is touched off with a wick. There are no wheels, flints, or steel to misfire. Treat it well, and it will not fail you." He gave instructions on how to take care of the weapon—washing out the barrel with boiling water, keeping the powder dry in rainy weather, how to measure a charge.

Finally he sent a man below to light a slow match. When he returned with the end aglow, Standish poured a charge of powder down the muzzle of the gun, slid in the ramrod, patted it gently home, and then dropped in a ball. He shook a few grains of black powder in the hole and put some more in the flashpan by its side. Then he screwed the glowing end of the slow match into the moveable arm, which would jerk the match down and dab the spark in the primed pan.

Suddenly John Billington's father cried out, "Get below! The tin soldier's going to blow us all to kingdom come!" Billington's friends laughed, and Standish gave him a sudden hard look. He cupped his powder-blackened hand around the flashpan, protecting the powder from the wind as he slid back the cover. In one smooth movement, he changed his position, gripped the gun with both hands, and squeezed the trigger. The wick jabbed down, and a little puffing explosion of muffled fire and black smoke hissed up out of the flashpan. A red belch of flame and sooty smoke followed from the muzzle. The heavy weapon bucked upward, and a cloud of soot and sulfur fumes drifted across the deck.

A few people started clapping, but Billington pretended to be shot. He grabbed his chest and cried out, "Captain Shrimp done me in!" It was the nickname given by most to Standish, but no one ever dared to use it to his face.

Standish put the weapon down, unbuckled his belt, and walked toward Billington. Standish was much shorter than the other man, but Billington suddenly turned white and backed up, crying, "Here, now! None of that!"

Standish stared at the bulky man as he took refuge behind some of the crowd. "If I hear but one more word, you won't like what I have in mind for you, Billington." Then he turned to face the rest of the crowd. "I'll have each of you men fire a shot. Come, now, and take your weapons."

Danny watched as the men went through the drill. "Dixie, what would they think if they saw a modern rifle? Or what about a machine gun?" Dixie didn't appear to be listening—her eyes were on Standish.

Constance moved closer and nudged him, "Go on, Danny. Ask if you can shoot."

Danny wanted to try it but was too shy to ask. He'd never shot a gun before. Captain Standish noticed him, and his tough face softened. "Come along! You'll have to learn someday, and now is as good a time as any. How old are you, and what's your name?"

"I'm Danny Fortune, Captain Standish. I'm fourteen."

"I wouldn't have guessed that," he said, apparently surprised. Danny was easily the taller of the two. "Well, let me see what you can do."

Danny took the weapon Standish handed him. "Can I shoot at a clay pigeon, sir?"

Standish smiled, saying, "Have a try, Danny."

As he prepared the weapon, he recognized Salterne's voice. "Look at the lubber now! Everybody go below or get shot!"

Danny flushed but paid no further attention. He had seen the others go through loading and priming the guns often enough, so he did that with little trouble. Then he swung the heavy weapon to his side and waited for Standish to toss the clay pigeon. The disc flew up and seemed to stand still in the air. "Shoot, Danny!" Standish yelled.

Danny swung the weapon upward, at the same time squeezing the trigger and keeping his hand cupped around the loose powder. As he squeezed the trigger, the wick jabbed down, and he lifted the gun in the general direction of the clay pigeon. The explosion kicked him backward so hard he sprawled on the deck.

Billington and his group burst out laughing, and Salterne made a cruel remark. But as the smoke from the musket cleared, Danny heard Constance cry out, "Look! The pigeon!"

Scrambling to his feet, he ran to the rail and saw shards of clay floating on the water. A round of enthusiastic applause went up, and Standish clapped his shoulder with a strong hand, his black eyes glowing with approval. "Good lad! I never saw a better shot in one so young!"

He gave a sharp look over his shoulder and announced, "Now, Mr. Billington, it's your turn. Let us see you knock down a pigeon or two!" When the man left muttering, Standish said so quietly that only Danny could hear it, "Your aim will be a help, Danny. I'd like to make you a sergeant—and I will, too, when the time comes!" He went away whistling.

Danny stood there as Dixie came up and gave him a hug, Constance following her example. "Oh, cut it out!" he blurted, beginning to feel a little self-conscious with all the attention. "It wasn't that great!"

"Don't belittle yourself, lad," Dr. Fuller said from behind. Danny turned around at the sound of his voice. "It was a marvelous shot—especially for a young fellow who's not done any shooting. You know what I'm thinking?" He stopped and took a long look at Danny. "I'm thinking it was a rare good fortune for you to come my way. No—it wasn't fortune at all!" He shook his head. "It was God's will."

Danny brushed his auburn hair back from his forehead. "I guess that's the truth, sir." Then he asked, "Are you afraid of what's ahead of us? You sure don't seem to be."

"Well, Danny, we don't know what lies ahead of us— and most people fear the unknown." He shrugged, adding, "Not all of us will survive, I'm sure. But a man can die for nothing, as most do, or he can die for something! That's where I and the other Saints stand. To others this is just a trip. It will lead to a better way of life, perhaps. But I've listened to our ministers long enough to believe that what we're doing is not just an accident. We're instruments in the hands of God!"

When he walked away, Constance sniffed. "Those people are always preaching! I don't think they believe in God any more than the rest of us. They're just stubborn and want to have their own way!"

Danny looked across the gray swells that seemed to go on forever. Dark clouds lay low in the west. "I don't know, Constance. But I think that before we get much farther, we're going to find out who really believes in God—and who doesn't!"

7

AS SEPTEMBER ADVANCED, the weather grew so cold that few of the passengers came up on the open deck unless they had to. The sky seemed to grow blacker every day, and the sea slid and shifted in mountainlike waves. Danny and his sister kept hoping for a glimpse of the Recall Unit, but they knew no more about its whereabouts than they had when they boarded the ship.

"Sooner or later we'll hear or see something," Danny said grimly. "There's nothing else like it in this century—whoever took it will brag about it or try to sell it."

The passengers stayed wrapped in blankets and extra clothing in the holds. Everyone was edgy and nervous. The crew had some heat from the galley flue and the captain his neat charcoal brazier, but the passengers had heat for only one hour every third morning. It was then that they were allowed to cook up their cauldron of porridge and stew on the charcoal brazier in the first hold.

It was September 15, and the children were gathered closely around the brazier's tiny fire. Danny and Dixie joined them. William Butten, Samuel Fuller's seventeen-year-old servant, was there too, looking ill and weak. He tried to move close to the warmth, but the fumes from the charcoal brought on a coughing fit, and he went below to rest on his cold bed.

"William's really sick," Dixie said with a worried expression. The boy was not very smart, and she was passing some of her time by trying to teach him how to read—a nearly hopeless task in Danny's opinion.

Danny agreed. William's illness did seem serious. "I asked Dr. Fuller about him, but he says he can't do anything to help. All this cold and wet—no wonder he's sick! It's a wonder we all don't have pneumonia."

"Have you heard any more about Salterne?" Dr. Fuller had told them that the brash young sailor who had knocked Danny down had fallen dangerously ill.

"John Clarke says he's dying," Danny said. He inched closer to the small brazier, trying to soak up as much of its heat as he could. "He used to make so much fun of sick people, calling them babies. Now he's screaming with pain."

"I know," Dixie answered. "And it's had an effect on the captain too. He never really trusted any of the Saints, but now that Dr. Fuller has offered to treat Salterne, he seems to have changed his mind."

"I think Salterne has appendicitis," Danny said. He had had his own appendix out four years ago, and the sharp pain of the attack was still fresh in his mind. "The doctor says he's tender on his right side and that he seems to be suffering from some kind of poison. If it is appendicitis, Salterne's going to die for sure. There isn't a doctor on earth right now who can take out an appendix!"

Dixie grew quiet for a minute, and she shuddered. "Just think, Danny. If you'd gotten appendicitis here instead of back home, you'd have died."

Danny nodded—that awful thought had already occurred to him several times. *Please, God, let us stay healthy,* he prayed. *Who knows what could happen to us if we got sick out here!*

Danny's guess proved to be right, for the next day Fuller announced gloomily, "Salterne died an hour ago. God rest his soul!"

The funeral was held that afternoon. The passengers gathered on deck, their cheeks chilled by the never-ending wind that whistled and sang through the ropes. The sea and sky were a dark slate color, and the ship was pushed forward by the steady, powerful winds.

Salterne's corpse lay wrapped in a piece of canvas on deck. Someone had placed a cannonball inside the canvas for weight and placed it on a board balanced on the edge of the ship. Captain Jones appeared from under the poop deck and stood before them holding a copy of the Book of Common Prayer. The crowd made a path for him as he walked to stand at the feet of the dead man. "All kneel!" he ordered.

Danny knew instantly that this command was directed at the Saints. They always stood to pray, believing it was superior to kneeling. The sailors knelt at once, but the Saints remained standing until finally Carver led the way. Soon all were kneeling.

"I am the resurrection and the life, saith the Lord: he that believeth in me, though he were dead, yet shall he live: and whosoever liveth and believeth in me shall never die. . . ."

The captain read at the top of his voice, and Danny took his eyes off him long enough to notice that long ribbons of clouds had begun to gather under the darkening sky. They were traveling very fast, and the blackness of the sky was now tinged with purple. The masts and wood around them were tinted with an eerie orange light. The wind's power increased with every passing second.

Captain Jones threw up his arm, saying, "And though after my skin worms destroy this body . . ." He was shouting now, and the sailor at his side was glancing up at the mainsail nervously.

Suddenly, the sun disappeared. Jones looked up, unable to read the print. The wind died down for a second. A wall of stone black clouds traveling from the east was swiftly overtaking the ship. The wind veered savagely— every sail became limp, then flapped wildly. The ship seemed to reel in the water, roughly throwing the passengers together.

Everyone dashed to get below as Jones shouted orders. He ordered Clarke to get six men to the mizzen lateen—then glanced back at Salterne's body, still poised on the board. He put his hand to its feet, shoved, and cried, "We commit this body to the sea!"

Wave after wave broke over the old ship, sending her reeling like a drunk. On the poop deck, Captain Jones continued to bellow orders: "Take in the spritsail. In with your topsails!"

Every inch of sail had to be furled. There was nothing to do but run before the wind, even though they were being driven hundreds of miles off course. Still the Atlantic pounded after them, foaming over the lower decks. The howling wind and pelting rain cut through the thin shirts and trousers of the sailors and drenched Danny to the core as he scrambled to get below deck.

It was a disaster below. Water ran everywhere—

through the hatch covers, under the two doors opening out onto the deck, and through many loosened seams in the main decking. Water trickled and seeped down from deck to deck, collecting in the bottom of the ship.

Danny peered through the darkness, searching for Dixie. Only the occasional glow of a candle lantern pierced the heavy black, making it difficult to see anything. Each roll of the ship seemed as though it might be the last.

Many of the women and children were crying. Suddenly, Danny spotted Dixie. She looked terrified. Their eyes met, and Danny raced over to Dixie and held on to her with all his might.

"Lord, do not let our people be lost!" William Bradford's voice rang out over the screaming wind. "Deliver us, as you delivered Jonah and Daniel!"

Then he raised his voice in a hymn. There in the darkness, the voices of others joined in:

> Jehovah feedeth me, I shall not lack
> In grassy folds he down doth make me lie
> He gently leads me quiet waters by
> He doth return my soul, for his name sake
> In paths of justice leads me quietly.

But still the wind thundered and the ocean smashed at the ship. Then, as their quaking voices began the next verse, a main beam cracked and buckled with a crash like a cannon-shot.

"Oh, God, save us! The ship is breaking up!" cried Dorothy Bradford, William Bradford's wife.

Her cry seemed to set off a frenzy of fear. Freezing water gushed in from the new openings in the splintered deck, and the terrified passengers huddled against the ship's sides to escape.

The crew rushed below and put their shoulders to the sagging beam to try to raise it. Instead, the massive beam sagged still more. Several sailors next brought up a spare beam from the hold, but they were not able to raise the damaged beam.

William Bradford and Edward Winslow were standing near Danny. The three watched anxiously. When all the crew's efforts seemed to fail, Bradford said, "Captain, we will go pray for you and your men."

Jones stared at him, his eyes steely in the thin light. He was soaked to the skin, and his curly black hair was matted. "Hoping for a miracle, are you?" he snapped. "Yes—you go ahead and pray—while my men and I *do* something!"

The captain's comment was clearly an insult, but Bradford and Winslow left the gun deck anyway, Danny tagging behind. Soon they had gathered most of the Saints to pray. John Alden and as many of the remaining strong men as could get under the massive beam did, straining and shoving, but nothing slowed its descent.

By one o'clock in the morning, the storm was falling away. Half a dozen lanterns had been brought in to help the crew see the damage it had done. It was apparent that sooner or later the beam would snap—when it did, the *Mayflower* would break in two.

"We'll have to turn back!" Stephen Hopkins shouted. His small face was twitching nervously, and he was not far from collapse.

"We've come too far," Jones snapped. "She'll never make it to the old world—or the new."

Bradford reentered at that moment. The captain, obviously upset over the danger to his ship, glared at him. "Well, where's your miracle?"

William Bradford did not flinch. "We have asked God to help you, Captain, and I believe He will do so. As we were praying, the words of Paul found in Acts 27:24 came to me: 'Fear not . . . God hath given thee all them that sail with thee.' "

"The next verse says, 'I believe God, that it shall be even as it was told me,' " added Winslow.

Captain Jones stared at them, then shook his head. "Very fine words—but they haven't fixed that beam!"

At that moment, the ship spun around, her side to the crested swells. Instantly, she was battered by an enormous wave that swept over the deck. Tons of water muffled the screams and cries of the people on board. Danny was flung so hard against the bulkhead his head rang.

The next thing he knew, John Alden was in front of the captain, shouting, "Captain! I know how we can brace that timber! We can—"

"Mind your business!" Clarke interrupted angrily, but Jones motioned for him to be quiet.

"What's your idea, Alden?"

"It just come to me, Captain Jones." He almost stuttered in his excitement. "I forgot it was there!"

"Forgot *what* was where?" Jones demanded.

"Why, when I was setting up my tools when I first come aboard, there was a big iron thing in my way—so I stowed it away to make room."

"What big iron thing?"

"It's a giant jack of some sort!" Alden cried. "The kind used for jacking up boats, I think."

"Go get it!" Jones shouted. "And *hurry*!"

Ten minutes later Alden was back, bearing the heavy jack in his powerful arms. An optimistic hubbub ran through the crowd, and Jones shouted, "Get it under the beam! Where's that timber, Mr. Clarke? We need all hands here!"

They laid a heavy timber down, put the jack on it, then balanced another timber on top. "Raise the jack!" Jones shouted. A cheer went up as the upright timber pressed against the beam, slowly pushing it up until it was back in place.

"That'll hold until calm weather," the carpenter said. "Then we'll spike a splint across that break and repeg it to the upper deck."

Suddenly William Bradford shouted, "The word of the Lord has come to pass! He has saved us!"

Captain Jones turned to study him. "Really, Mr. Bradford, I think John Alden deserves *some* credit." Then, with a gleam in his gray eyes, he asked, "Elder Bradford, why do you think God would use a Stranger such as John Alden to save us with so many Saints around?"

Bradford's expression was strained, but he replied evenly, "I am not as certain as I once was about some things, Captain. But I *am* certain God has delivered us." He gave the captain a gentle smile and asked, "Can't you say 'amen' to that, sir?"

All eyes looked curiously at Captain Jones. He had told everyone that he thought the Saints were fanatics, and they were wondering how he would respond. He nodded shortly. "Amen, then, Elder Bradford. And God be thanked!"

The storm died down that night. The next day at noon, Mrs. Stephen Hopkins gave birth to a boy. Constance came to where Danny and Dixie were standing above deck and told them the news. "I've got a new baby brother," she announced. "Come see."

They followed her down into the darkened hold to view the newest addition to the Hopkins family. "How precious!" Dixie crooned. "Can I hold him?"

She took the newborn in her arms and exclaimed over his perfect fingernails and pudgy cheeks. "Look, Danny! Isn't he perfect?"

Danny was not impressed. He wanted to say the baby looked like six pounds of raw hamburger but knew that would not go over very well. He leaned forward and declared loudly, "Now *that's* a baby!" Danny knew that would please the parents without committing him to anything. "What's his name?"

"Oceanus!" Constance said proudly. "Isn't that positively elegant!"

"Well, it's sure *different*," Danny acknowledged. "He won't ever be confused with someone else—not with an 'elegant' name like that!"

After a few minutes he pried himself loose from Constance and returned to the deck with Dixie. They didn't say much at first—just stood there staring out into the miles of sea that surrounded them. Finally Danny broke the silence. "How are you doing, Dixie? Really, I mean."

She dropped her head and looked down at her hands. "I worry a lot about Mom and Jimmy. We've been gone for weeks. Mom must be a basket case by now! And Jimmy—I just hope he hasn't gotten sicker now that we're missing too! We should never have agreed to do this."

"Maybe she's asked Mordecai and Zacharias if they've seen us," Danny said, trying to be hopeful. "I mean, she *must* have gotten the certified check by now."

"But she wouldn't know it came from them," Dixie protested. "You addressed the envelope, and you never mentioned going to see them."

"But it'll be postmarked Mayville, and it will have the name of our great-uncles' bank on it. Who else would it be from? Maybe the police will put two and two together and . . ." Actually he had thought about all this many times but disguised his own doubts. Their great-uncles weren't likely to step forward to admit what they had done with their young relatives. Zacharias and Mordecai certainly weren't the type to risk a prison sentence.

Suddenly Danny said, "Dixie, I know neither of us have done much praying, but—"

She looked up at him as if she sensed what he was thinking. "I know. You're thinking about John Alden finding that jack, right?"

"Well, it can't be a coincidence, can it?" he asked. "Elder Bradford prayed—and John remembered the jack."

She nodded slowly, but then her eyes dimmed. "But, Danny, how can we ask God for anything? We certainly haven't been on good terms with Him."

"Well, I don't know much about God, but I don't think it works quite like that. He doesn't hold out on us until we're good. He just wants us to admit that He's the only one who can help us. Then if we pray . . ."

The wind was still moaning, and the sound seemed to discourage Dixie. "Just think, though—a few days ago I was griping about my stupid teeth! And I thought *they* were a major problem!"

"I guess whatever problem we have at the moment

seems important to us." Danny shrugged. "Right now I'm as worried about Mom and Jimmy back home—and Dad, wherever he is—as I am about us here. Do you think we could sort of ask God to help them?"

She nodded slowly. "I will if you will. But you'll have to do the praying out loud. I wouldn't know where to start."

He swallowed hard, feeling shy and slightly embarrassed. "I guess I'll do it then—but don't expect anything fancy."

Danny bowed his head. "God," he began. "I know we don't have any right to ask you for anything. But we don't know where else to turn, so we're asking anyway. Will you take care of Mom and Jimmy—and Dad too. And help us to get home again." He tried to say more, but a thick lump rose in his throat and tears stung his eyes. "I guess that's all, God," he whispered.

"Amen!" Dixie said. She squeezed his hand hard. Danny looked at her and smiled, then turned to look out over the rail. But what he saw was not the Atlantic Ocean, but faces from another place and time—the faces of his family and friends back home.

8

DURING THE TWELVE WEEKS of the voyage, the Fortune twins had gotten to know everyone on board the small, bobbing world of the *Mayflower*. Indeed, it would have been hard *not* to, so tightly were they packed into the ship. The division between the Saints and the Strangers grew wider as time passed, making life difficult for Danny and Dixie, who spent time with both groups. Stephen Hopkins, Constance's father, was one of the leaders of the Strangers. The Strangers at first seemed suspicious of the twins, but as the days passed, they simply ignored them.

"The Strangers aren't so bad," Danny reflected. "Mr. Billington is pretty rough, I guess—but Mr. Mullins is just as nice as any of the Saints."

"I guess so," Dixie said cautiously. She was trying to make a blouse, and it was not going well. "I'll never learn to sew!" she snapped after pricking her finger for the tenth time that day. She nursed her finger for a moment, then changed the subject. "Danny, have you noticed anything different about the Strangers recently?"

"Like what?" he asked quickly. "Well, actually, now that you mention it . . . they do seem to be cooking up something."

Dixie nodded. "Several times I've walked up on a group of them. When one man spots me and motions to the others, right away they change the subject." She took another cautious stitch, then shook her head. "I hope there isn't going to be trouble."

"I heard Mr. Bradford talking to Dr. Fuller," Danny said. "I think the Saints have guessed something's up but can't figure out what it is."

Dixie got up. "I'm going to ask Mrs. Bradford to help me with this stupid thing. I'm making a mess out of it!" She turned to leave, then paused. "Danny, I've noticed that she's not happy—Mrs. Bradford, I mean."

"Well, this voyage *is* rough." He shrugged. "And she seems sort of delicate. I don't think she's been through many hard times."

"She's definitely used to better things," Dixie agreed. "Most of the other women have learned to at least put up with the hardships, but Dorothy Bradford just gets more miserable every day." She gathered up her sewing, saying, "I'll go talk to her awhile. Why don't you come with me?"

They made their way down the steep steps to the main deck, where they were spotted by John Billington Jr. "Dixie! Danny!" He smiled, coming up to take Dixie's arm. "I've been looking for you."

Dixie returned his smile. "I'm going to get Mrs. Bradford to help me make this blouse," she said, "and Danny's going to keep me company." Then in a teasing voice she suggested, "I'm sure she'd give you a sewing lesson, John."

He stared at her and laughed shortly. "Not likely! Why would a man need to know how to sew? Look, let's go to the galley instead. Cook is making food for the crew. He likes pretty girls—maybe you can charm him out of some for Danny and me."

The idea sounded good to Danny, and they started toward the galley.

"I don't know about me charming the cook, John." Dixie gave him a sideways glance. "It would take someone like Priscilla Mullins to do that."

"She's a handsome one, right enough!" John nodded enthusiastically. "She's got John Alden moonstruck, if you've noticed."

"I guess everyone has noticed," Danny grinned. "But he's too shy to do anything about it. Her father has lots of money, and John's just a hired hand."

"Yes, but when a woman likes a fellow, she can usually get him," John observed. "And knowing Priscilla's father, he'll give in. Who wouldn't want to make a girl like that happy?" They had passed into the small space that separated the first hold from the galley, but the cook was nowhere to be seen. It would never do to just take food without asking—not with this hungry crew to deal with.

John left them to find his father, and the twins made their way along the crowded passageway to the small cubicle that had been assigned to the leaders of the Saints. When Dixie knocked on the door, a man's voice said, "Come in." They stepped in and found William Bradford and his wife, Dorothy, inside.

"Oh . . ." Dixie said quickly, turning to go. "We didn't mean to disturb you." Danny felt awkward and wished he had remained on deck.

"Come in, children," Bradford said. His face looked troubled, but his voice was kind. "I've been meaning to have a talk with you. There, Dixie, sit down by Mrs. Bradford."

Danny was intimidated by Bradford. He wasn't a

frightening man, but he was very intelligent, and Danny was fearful that he or Dixie would say something to give away their secret.

But Bradford didn't seem the least suspicious. He asked about their past, and somehow Danny managed to squeak by without lying, telling him that there had been a tragedy and they had "lost" their parents. "You poor children!" Bradford exclaimed. "But at least you have each other . . . and the Lord." He paused, examining them with his deep-set eyes, "And do you know God, Danny and Dixie Fortune?"

The question didn't surprise Danny—all the Saints, especially Bradford and Brewster, felt themselves responsible for the passengers' spiritual condition. The twins nodded hesitantly, and Danny admitted, "We've always gone to church, but it hasn't really meant that much to us, Mr. Bradford. But I know we've both thought about God a lot—especially since leaving England."

Bradford gave them a friendly smile. "Quite understandable. I am willing to help you with any questions you might have," he added. "I have a meeting now with Elder Brewster, but perhaps later?"

"Yes, sir. Thank you," the twins said in unison.

The man turned and said, "Why don't you keep my wife company while I go to my meeting?"

As soon as he was gone, Dixie said, "I was going to ask you to help me with this sewing, Mrs. Bradford—but I can come back later if you don't feel well."

Dorothy Bradford looked ill as she sat bent over on the edge of the cot. Her already fair skin seemed even paler, and her large blue eyes were wild. She shook her head. "Come—sit down, Danny." Her voice was monotone, and she waved Danny toward the chair near the bed. "Sewing will give me something to do." Mrs. Bradford took the cloth from Dixie and examined it with her graceful fingers.

"You have such pretty hands, Mrs. Bradford!" Dixie complimented her.

The woman held one hand up to study it, then said abruptly, "Before this mad voyage is over, they'll be nothing but claws!" Her harsh words shocked Danny and Dixie both, but Mrs. Bradford sat there, unaware. She began to speak in a low tone, telling of her wonderful life in Leyden, Holland—her beautiful home, her friends. Before Leyden she had lived in her father's house in England, where she'd had everything a young girl could possibly want.

No wonder this trip is so hard on her, Danny thought. *I'm surprised she agreed to come at all.*

Mrs. Bradford's voice was filled with such miserable longing that Danny couldn't think of anything to say. Finally, when Mrs. Bradford stopped, Dixie tried reassuring her. "Your life in Europe sounds very nice. I'm sure it was hard to give up, but maybe when you get settled in the New World it won't—"

"Get settled!" Mrs. Bradford exclaimed sharply, her eyes snapping with anger. "We'll never 'get settled' in that wilderness! What's waiting for us? Savage beasts and people just as savage! No friends to greet us—no homes—nothing!"

Suddenly she threw the sewing down and fell on her face on the cot. Ragged sobs shook her shoulders. Danny indicated to Dixie that they should leave, and his sister stood up, saying, "I'll come back later, Mrs. Bradford."

There was no answer. Danny left the cabin feeling depressed. Dixie said she wanted to rest for a while, so Danny went in search of Constance Hopkins. She at least was always cheerful and fun to be around. He found her in the section of the main deck where her family had staked out their crowded space. She waved for Danny to join her, and soon they were busy talking.

Danny didn't notice when it started, but eventually he became aware that some sort of meeting was going on down the deck. He recognized the loud bullying tones of John Billington Sr. and the quieter voice of Stephen Hopkins. Constance seemed to be unaware of what the men were saying, but Danny began to eavesdrop even as Constance rambled on about her past—mostly about other boys she had liked.

"I tell you, it won't do!" John Billington went on angrily, "Them precious *Saints*—they ain't goin' to lord it over John Billington! You can bet on that!"

Stephen Hopkins spoke up, his thin voice almost a whine. "Well now, John, who says they are?"

Christopher Martin's sharp and angry voice broke in. "*They* say so, that's who. They managed to worm their way in—they got rid of my authority as soon as we got aboard the ship, didn't they? Who used to be governor but me! Do you think it'll be any different when we get ashore? Not by my reckoning!"

"Martin's right!" Billington snapped. "And I ain't goin' to stand for it!"

Hopkins said quickly, "Wait now—we don't want to start anything on board the ship. You've all seen how Bradford has the captain eating out of his hand." He lowered his voice. "Remember—I've been through this once before."

"How's that?" Martin demanded.

"Why, I was with Sir William Gates back in 1609," Hopkins boasted. "We was going to Virginia to make a colony, we was. But a storm wrecked us off Bermuda, and Gates tried to make slaves out of us! But I'd have none of it—not Stephen Hopkins."

"What did you do?" Billington demanded.

"Do? Why, I led a revolt!" A rumble ran around the men who were listening, and Hopkins said proudly, "I waited my chance, and as soon as I could get a few good chaps, why, we went at it. We told Sir William Gates what he could do with his authority!"

"I heard of that," Billington said, laughing shortly. "All of you who rebelled was put to a court-martial, ain't that right, Hopkins? Way I heard it, every man jack of 'em was hanged—except *you*!"

"Well, that was the way of it," Hopkins admitted, but he sounded unconcerned as he continued. "It won't be that way this time. There's a lot more of *us* than there is of them!"

Angry talk ran around the group, then Billington said, "There's maybe something to what you say, Hopkins. But we'll say nothing—not 'til we're off this ship and on land. *Then* we'll see how Mr. William Bradford's authority lasts!"

Steps sounded and the men moved closer. Suddenly nervous, Danny looked straight at Constance and began babbling. He had no idea what he was saying. He felt rather than saw someone pause to stand behind him.

"Yes, sir?" Constance asked. "What is it?"

Danny stopped talking and turned to look into the unfriendly face of John Billington Sr., who was eyeing him suspiciously. Danny smiled brightly and said in as casual a tone as he could manage, "Oh, hello, Mr. Billington. Constance and I were just having a visit. You can't expect a young man like me to stay away from the prettiest girl on the ship, can you?"

Billington glared at him, and Danny thought for one frightening moment that the man was going to hit him. But Billington grunted, turned, and left. Constance appeared not to have noticed anything. As soon as he could, Danny left to seek out Dixie.

She was trying again to work on her half-finished blouse and happy for the interruption. When he told her what he had heard, her expression grew serious. "We have to tell someone," she said instantly. "Maybe Dr. Fuller."

Danny agreed—despite his gruffness when they had first met him, Dr. Fuller had proved to be someone they could trust. They searched until they found him near the bow. He turned and greeted them, and Danny immediately told him what he had heard. The doctor stood there, his dark eyes fixed on Danny's face as he related the incident. "Good work, son! We've suspected there was some sort of trouble brewing. Thanks to you, we know now what it is."

Danny hesitated, then asked, "Sir, I've been wondering—how are so many different people going to get along well enough to build a town? It doesn't look to me like it will work."

Fuller pulled his beard and gave Danny a brief smile. "Some of us have been asking ourselves the same question, my boy. And the answer is that we have to keep some kind of order. We have to learn how to live together—and we're going to need rules to do it."

"It doesn't sound like the Strangers are interested in

rules—some of them, at least," Dixie ventured.

"No," the doctor agreed, "but it's a big country we're going to—bigger than any of us have ever known. If any of us are going to survive these first few years, we've all got to work together." He shrugged his heavy shoulders, a strange mixture of doubt and hope in his eyes. "It'll take a miracle, I'm thinking. But it's a miracle we've gotten this far. God's not going to forsake us as long as we're His." Then he added, "I'll tell the others what you've told me. Keep your ears open and your mouths closed for now."

"Yes, sir." They both nodded. When the doctor had left them alone, Dixie said, "I didn't think it would be like this, Danny. Not on the *Mayflower*."

"I know," he answered. "I guess I always thought life in the past was easier—that people got along better than they do in our time." He watched the prow cut through the gray water and said, "Remember how I used to love to watch movies about the Knights of the Round Table? I always imagined the days of jousting and castles and stuff were so cool."

"You don't watch that kind of movie much anymore, do you?"

"Nope." Danny laughed. "One day I read a history book about what those days were *really* like. Suddenly they didn't seem so great anymore."

"Didn't they have a lot of contests where knights climbed on horses and ran at each other with pointed lances?"

"Oh sure, they had plenty of contests," he nodded. "But in the movies, the horses are always so fast—like race horses. It wasn't like that at all. Knights were big men, and they put on heavy suits of armor—not to mention all the armor they put on the *horses*. It was important to have the biggest, strongest horses they could. So instead of having two lightning-fast horses racing toward each other at full speed, they had two huge farm-type horses lumbering forward at about a mile an hour. Some excitement, huh?"

"But what about the dances and the women with their pretty dresses?"

"Oh, they had balls and pretty clothes. But they also didn't have dry cleaners to clean their clothes—and no bathtubs, either!" Danny grinned at Dixie—life on the *Mayflower* had quickly taught them the smelly realities of life without showers or bathtubs. "Imagine several hundred people who haven't had a bath in months wearing clothes that have *never* been washed, eating food that's probably half rotten because there was no way to keep it fresh. It would smell pretty *ripe*, don't you think?"

Dixie frowned. "I liked it better before I knew all that! I'd rather think about those days being nice and romantic!"

"You've always wanted everything to be romantic," Danny teased her. "Life just isn't that way. I mean, look at the life we've been living—the food we've been eating, always wearing the same clothes—it isn't exactly romantic. Who would have guessed that the Pilgrims would be so dirty!"

"They're dirty all right." She looked around the deck with a smile. "The whole group stinks! But if they'd stayed behind in England because they were afraid of a little dirt, there wouldn't have been any United States!"

"That's true enough," Danny said thoughtfully. "I wonder what Mrs. Simpkins, my history teacher, would think about the real Pilgrims. She called them failures once, saying new frontiers are always settled by failures. She said successful people stay where they are because they're comfortable. It's the people who've failed that go to new places, hoping things will go better there."

"I don't know about that," Dixie responded. "Mr. Bradford sure isn't a failure! He had a nice house and all sorts of beautiful things. Remember what Mrs. Bradford told us?"

"Yeah, I know. That's what's *different* about this frontier. These people—the Saints, anyway—aren't going to the New World to get rich and make lots of money. A lot of them were already successful in that way in Europe. They're giving up a good life so they can worship God the way they want to."

Danny stood there, thinking about the Saints and how different they were from the Strangers.

"Danny," Dixie interrupted his thoughts, "What if one of the crew took the Recall Unit? He'd keep it, wouldn't he? Until he got back to England, that is. Then he could sell it."

"I've been thinking about that," Danny admitted. "But we can't exactly go through their things. Some of the crew are always around, and if they caught us—it'd be ugly." He gave Dixie a quick pat on the shoulders. "Well, we've told God our problems. And you remember what Elder Brewster said in his sermon last Sunday?"

"I remember," she nodded. "He said, 'God will give us a miracle if we believe Him, but we have to leave the *why* and the *how* up to Him.'" She looked at Danny and said, "It's hard to do that, isn't it?"

"Yeah, it is—but it's the only way to go, Dixie. So let's keep praying—and keep hoping that God will help us find that Recall Unit!"

9

NOVEMBER CAME, AND THOUGH DANNY could feel the ship moving through the water, the horizon never changed. It forever remained the same imprisoning circle, and the sameness was wearing on the *Mayflower*'s passengers. Dorothy Bradford in particular became more depressed as the days went on. "We'll never see land again, you know," she announced one day to the twins. "We'll all die at sea." She looked down into the wake of the *Mayflower* and whispered, "It would not be bad to die in the sea."

It was clear to everyone on board that all joy and hope had left Mrs. Bradford. And life was no better for poor William Butten, who became thinner and sicker almost by the hour. Danny had learned to like William. Danny spent many hours by his side, even though the boy was simple and hung on those who cared for him. Danny read to him out of one of Dr. Fuller's few history books, and though William seemed to understand little of it, he never tired of listening.

Once when Danny was reading, Elder Brewster came to sit beside them. He listened as Danny read. When the chapter was ended, he said, "How is it with you, my dear boy?"

At fifty-four, Brewster was the oldest of the Saints. He had sharp features, kind brown eyes, and his brown hair and beard were shot with gray. He was not a preacher, Danny had discovered. Brewster was merely an elder, but being the closest thing to a minister the Saints now had, they honored him as such. William held out a weak, bony hand, saying, "I'm fine, Elder Brewster. Danny always makes me feel better." Then he asked the question he asked every day, "Do you think I'll be better soon?"

"I pray daily that you will be, my boy," Brewster returned. He prayed again right there, and when he was finished he sat back and was silent.

Danny asked, "How did you happen to join up with the Saints, Elder Brewster?"

"Why, it's a long story," Brewster smiled. "But then we're in no hurry, are we?" He began to speak, describing how a group of Christians had broken off from the Church of England because they believed it was corrupt. They were called "Separatists" because they had separated from the official state church—which was illegal to do in those days. William Brewster had held secret Separatist meetings in his home in Scrooby, where he was in charge of the postal service. A congregation had grown up there, William Bradford among them. In 1607 Brewster lost his job because of his religious beliefs, and the group had migrated to Holland.

"We found it possible to worship peacefully in Leyden." Brewster stroked his beard.

"Why didn't you all stay there?" Danny asked.

"For several reasons," Brewster said. "For one thing, it seemed likely Spain would attack Holland. If they won, we'd be forced to become Catholics—that would never do. We don't believe in all those rituals or in obeying popes and bishops. Just as bad, we found our young people taking up the loose moral habits of the young people of Holland." A smile touched his lips as he said quietly, "And if the King of England had found me, he would have cut off my head."

"What for?"

"He thought I was the man printing books that attacked the Church of England. That is a capital offense in England."

"And were you?" Danny asked in amazement.

Brewster laughed and got to his feet. "Better if you don't know the answer to that, young fellow—just in case it ever comes to a trial. This way you won't have to say I confessed to such a thing." He leaned over and patted William on the shoulder. "I'll be back to see you tomorrow, my boy. Don't lose heart. You'll see the New World, I feel sure."

After Brewster left, William became upset. His face was so thin that his eyes looked enormous, and his flesh had been burned off by the fever he could not shake. "I'm thinking I'll not see the New World," he mumbled sadly.

Danny tried to cheer him up, but it was no use. Eventually the boy fell into a restless sleep. Getting to his feet, Danny went to the deck and joined Constance, who gave his hand a little squeeze. "I'm hoping to be the first to see the New World," she said. She moved closer to him and whispered, "We're sweethearts, aren't we, Danny?"

Danny felt embarrassed when she said things like that—he had no plans to remain in the 1600s just to be with Constance. He rolled his eyes. "I guess so."

"Well, why don't you ever hold my hand?" she demanded.

"Constance, there are people on deck!" he said, looking around. "They might see us."

"And what difference does that make?"

"It would make a difference to your father, for one thing," Danny pointed out. "He'd take the hide off me."

"I don't care what *he* thinks," she said, obviously frustrated. She stamped her foot, her eyes sparking. "You're around those Saints so much, you're becoming as holy and prudish as they are!" she shouted and, whirling around, she left him standing there.

"Having a little quarrel with your girl, eh, Danny?" Danny turned quickly to see John Alden rising from behind a mass of sailing gear. He walked up beside Danny. "Women are a puzzle to me. I can do most anything with a piece of wood—cut it to size, plane it, bend it by using steam. I always *know* what that wood's going to do. But women—well . . ." He paused and pushed out his lips in an exasperated gesture. "There's only *one* thing you can count on as far as a woman's concerned!"

"What's that, John?"

"Why, to do just what you don't expect!"

Danny smiled to himself; it was clear John was referring to Priscilla Mullins. As much as he liked her, John always seemed a little tongue-tied and unsure of himself around the beautiful young woman. *But that will change soon enough!* Danny thought.

An idea suddenly came to Danny. "Say, John—can I ask you something—just between us?"

"'Course you can!"

"Well, I've lost something," Danny began carefully. "To tell the truth, I think somebody took it." He described the Recall Unit, then asked, "Have you seen anything like that?"

"No, can't say as I have," Alden murmured. "And it

sounds like the sort of trinket a man wouldn't forget if he saw it."

"Well, if you do see it, tell me, will you?" Danny asked. "It means a lot to me and Dixie. It was a gift . . . from our uncles."

It was only two days later that Danny saw John Alden take a deep breath, walk up to Priscilla Mullins, and say, "Ah . . . good morning, miss." He looked like a man going to be hanged, he was so nervous. But when the pretty Priscilla turned and looked at John with a surprised smile, he came to himself at once.

Danny grinned as he left the deck where the two were standing together talking. But his smile vanished when he met Dr. Fuller coming up from below deck. "What's wrong, sir?" Danny asked.

"William is dying," he answered sadly. "Nothing I can do for the boy—never has been." He gave his head a heavy shake, saying, "I'm going for Elder Brewster. Go sit with him, Danny."

Danny found William unconscious, his breathing so faint that at first Danny thought he was already dead. But then he began tossing. After Brewster arrived, Danny sat to one side with Dixie, who came as soon as she had heard the news. All night long the passengers prayed and waited; young William Butten had been a favorite with everyone.

Morning came and he lived on, but there was no hope of recovery. Danny and Dixie choked down a few bites of breakfast and went to sit on deck. The day was cold, and a hard wind had been whipping the sails all night. The misery of the cold and the gloom brought on by the long voyage—now capped by William's illness—settled on them like a weight.

"Danny!" Dixie murmured, her teeth chattering from the cold. "I'm so tired of all this!" She rested her arms on the rail and laid her head down.

Danny put his hand on her shoulder. "Me too. But it'll get better. We've *got* to find land soon. I just wish I could remember when the *Mayflower* landed. And I thought history class would never come in handy!" He got up and began to stamp his feet hard to restore the feeling in his numb toes. Suddenly he stopped stock still, then bent over. "Dixie! Look at this!"

"What is it?"

"It's a dead bird! It looks like some kind of sparrow—the kind of bird that would never be out far at sea. We've got to be close to land!" He peered through the heavy mist that surrounded the ship but couldn't see anything. "It must have been blown into the rigging last night or this morning. Come on—let's show it to Captain Jones!"

They raced along the main deck, climbed to the poop deck, and found the captain staring blankly in the fog. "Captain Jones!" Danny cried. "Look—a sparrow! I just found it on deck!"

Jones wheeled and inspected the tiny, bedraggled bird in Danny's hands. A smile broke the stern look on his face. "Bless God!" he exclaimed. "We're there! We made it!"

He called to Clarke, and the two of them began excitedly to make calculations. Dixie said enthusiastically, "Let's go tell the others, Danny. They'll be so happy!"

They raced down the ladder and found Mr. Bradford. When they told him the good news, he exclaimed, "It's the hand of God! I must go tell Dorothy at once! This will make her better!"

As he left, Dixie said, "I hope the news *will* do Mrs. Bradford good, Danny. She's almost out of her mind. Sometimes she sits for hours just staring at the wall."

"She'll get better once we get off this boat," Danny reassured her. "We all will!"

They spread the word quickly, and soon the entire company was on the deck, each one hoping to be the first to spot land.

Finally Danny said, "Come on, Dixie. Let's go tell William."

The sick boy was only half awake, but he tried to look up when Dixie said, "Look, William."

"What is it?" he whispered.

"It's a bird," she said, holding it out for him to touch. "It's a sparrow from the New World—the first one we've seen. We are very close to the New World now. We'll be seeing it any time!"

"Can I go up and see it, do you think?" he asked.

"Well, it's pretty cold on deck," Danny said quickly. "We'll have to talk to Dr. Fuller. But I don't see why not. As soon as we spot land, I'll come and get you if he says we can."

"I don't think it could hurt the poor boy," Fuller said sadly when Danny told him about William's request a few minutes later. "He's too far gone. As soon as we sight land, I'll carry him up myself."

But that never happened. For sometime early the next morning William crawled from his bed and made his way to the deck. As soon as his disappearance was discovered, a search was made. He was found in the bows, trembling with cold. "I been looking," he said to the burly doctor as he was carried below. "I been looking for the New World, Dr. Fuller. And I seen it—right over there!"

"Did you, William?" Dr. Fuller asked gently as he put the thin body back into the bunk and covered it. "What was it like?"

"Oh, it was beautiful!" Butten whispered. "Green grass and a warm sun! And there was grapes growing and lots of trees! Oh, it's a fair land, the New World!"

An hour later, William began coughing. He died holding Elder Brewster's hand. "Dear, dear boy!" the old man wept. "He's gone to the *real* New World!"

That afternoon, Captain Jones read the funeral service over William Butten's body. When the canvas sack was dropped into the ocean, the boy went to his watery grave with the dead bird in his hand.

The next morning dawned cold and windless. The sky was an inverted gray bowl. Without the wind, the ship was unable to move forward. "I'd like to get out and *push*!" Danny said in irritation.

Suddenly a cry came from above their heads, "Land ho! Land ho!"

"Whereabouts?" Captain Jones yelled.

"On the weather!"

Jones and Clarke turned at once with their telescopes, and every eye followed their direction. Danny strained his eyes but could see nothing. The whispering breeze feathered the surface of the water, and a fog scudded along the surface. He stared until his eyes burned, and then—finally—the horizon broke. "There!

Over there, Dixie!" he shouted.

A tiny smudge interrupted the horizon—a horizon that had been unbroken for two months. He stood there, amazed, as Captain Jones and Clarke began screaming at the sailors to put on all sail.

"Well, we made it to the New World," Dixie said, tears in her eyes. She gave a brief smile. "At least we're back in our own country—even if we are a few hundred years early!"

10

THEY HAD BEEN SAILING for sixty-six long days when they spotted land—the sight of it had never made Danny happier. They were close enough to see high brown bluffs and the tops of tall trees, but they could not find a safe place to anchor.

"We'll find a harbor tomorrow," Captain Jones said. But although he nudged the ship along the next day, they were no closer to getting off.

During this time, Bradford and the Saints' leaders busily planned for the coming days. When a group of Strangers led by Billington demanded a hearing, they were caught off guard.

"We ain't satisfied with the way things is going, Mr. Bradford," Billington said bluntly. "And we've come to inform you that when we get ashore, we intend to exercise our own liberty."

"That's right!" Stephen Hopkins piped up, his face twitching with excitement. He glared at Bradford, adding, "There's none with the power to command us—not if we land at this spot."

"And why not?" Bradford asked.

"Because this ain't Virginia, like we signed for."

Danny knew Bradford was aware of this fact—he had heard the man ask Captain Jones about their location. "That is so. The charter calls for us to settle south of latitude forty-one. But we are hundreds of miles north of the Hudson River, and Captain Jones informs me that to beat our way down there would be very dangerous. He also wants to get the ship back to England as soon as possible."

"What it comes to," Carver said quickly, "is that we really have only two choices—settle here, or go back to England."

"We signed for Virginia!" Hopkins said stubbornly. "And if we stay here, we ain't under your authority."

"It's all Virginia as far as I'm concerned," Bradford said.

"We'll elect our own governor," Hopkins threatened.

"And you'll be a candidate, I assume?" Edward Winslow asked sarcastically. "I will point out that you tried this once before—though your friends may not be aware of it. You were once found guilty of mutiny and rebellion. Isn't that so?"

Hopkins had been cornered. "Yes," he muttered. Several of the men looked at him in shock.

"I didn't know that," William Mullins said. "I'll have nothing to do with a mutineer!"

Other men spoke up in agreement, and Bradford said instantly, "We'll have no more of this! Mr. Carver, Mr. Brewster—come with me. The rest of you hold yourselves ready for a meeting within the next few hours."

The three men spent the rest of the day in the Captain's Great Cabin. The ship was buzzing with rumors. A night passed, and on the following morning Bradford called for a meeting of the leaders.

The Great Cabin was crowded, packed with most of the men on board the ship. Danny had squeezed in along with Dr. Fuller and found a tight corner where he could see everything. The faces of the leaders were gray with strain.

"We must all learn to get along in the new land," Brewster began. "Some sort of terms must be offered to all—Saints and Strangers alike. We will need a written document that sets forth the idea that everyone will have fair treatment under the new government. To that end, we have prepared a compact—an agreement—which I will ask Brother Bradford to read."

Bradford waited until the room grew quiet, then in a steady voice read the *Mayflower Compact*.

IN the Name of God, Amen. We, whose names are underwritten, the Loyal Subjects of our dread Sovereign Lord King *James*, by the Grace of God, of *Great Britain*, *France*, and *Ireland*, King, *Defender of the Faith*, etc. Having undertaken for the Glory of God, and Advancement of the Christian Faith, and the Honour of our King and Country, a Voyage to plant the first colony in the northern Parts of Virginia; Do by these Presents, solemnly and mutually in the Presence of God and one another, covenant and combine ourselves together into a civil Body Politick, for our better Ordering and Preservation, and Furtherance of the Ends aforesaid; And by Virtue hereof do enact, constitute, and frame, such just and equal Laws, Ordinances, Acts, Constitutions, and Offices, from time to time, as shall be thought most meet and convenient for the general Good of the Colony; unto which we promise all due Submission and Obedience. In WITNESS whereof we have hereunto subscribed our names at *Cape Cod* the eleventh of *November*, in the Reign of our Sovereign Lord King *James* of *England*, *France*, and *Ireland*, the eighteenth and of *Scotland*, the fifty-fourth. *Anno Domini*, 1620.

"This will be the foundation of our government,"

Bradford said quietly. He put the paper on the captain's desk, picked up a quill, and signed it. Those men who had the highest social status—that of master—stepped up, led by John Carver. Both Saints and Strangers were included in this group of twelve.

Next the goodmen—the next social rank below master—were invited to sign. Twenty-seven of these signed; then four servants signed on orders from the masters. In the end forty-one of the sixty-five men on board signed the *Mayflower Compact*. The women, unfortunately, were excluded. The twins had quickly learned that seventeenth-century English law treated women more like property than people.

"We will now elect a governor to serve for one year," Bradford announced. He looked straight at Hopkins and Billington, daring them to speak. "I offer the name of John Carver."

"I second that name," William Brewster said quickly. Almost before he knew it, John Carver became the first popularly elected official in the New World!

Most of the men left the Great Cabin, but Danny lingered with Dr. Fuller and a few others. Captain Jones had said nothing during the meeting, but now he commented, "This is an unusual thing, Mr. Bradford—a civil body politic. The king would not want common people running their own government—nor electing governors. The king has always appointed the governors."

Bradford gave the captain a smile. "It is the way we choose our pastors—by popular vote."

"Well, *that* doesn't sit too well with King James, either," Jones laughed, "as you well know. Why were you not elected? You are the natural leader of the group."

Bradford seemed uncomfortable. "Mr. Carver is not

as . . . as *direct* as I am. He will be better suited to the position."

"And *you* will be the real power behind him," Jones said with a grin. "But having elections is a dangerous practice! What if the men elect a man who is not able, or who is dishonest?"

"Why, then they will elect a better man to replace him!"

Captain Jones shook his head. "It will never work, sir, this democracy of yours. People must have a king—the English at least."

"Time will tell, Captain Jones," Bradford said. "I think English people have begun to lose their taste for rule by kings. Freedom is in the air."

"It sure is!" Danny piped up without meaning to. They all looked at him in surprise, having forgotten he was there. Suddenly feeling out of place, Danny ducked his head and dashed out of the cabin. He found Dixie talking to John Billington.

"Boy, when we get home again, will I have a report to give in history class! I've just seen the signing of the *Mayflower Compact*!"

John stared at him blankly, "Where is home, Danny? You've never said. And why would you want to return when we can live in the New World?"

Danny pointed toward the west. "Home's over that way, John."

John shook his head and laughed. "Ain't nothing over that way but wild Indians."

Danny grinned and shrugged. "Maybe that's so, but it's still my home," he said, then changed the subject. "I'll be glad when we find a harbor. I'm dying to get my feet on solid land!"

✹　✹　✹

"I don't think we're *ever* going to get off this old boat!" Dixie wailed.

Danny looked at his sister, who was huddled close to the galley fire. "It looks that way," he agreed wearily. "I thought we'd spot land, pile off the boat, and start building a settlement. But here it is a month since we've reached land, and the leaders are *still* trying to make up their minds about where to build the town."

The twins moved to the deck to watch the men get ready to go on their second expedition that month with the *Mayflower*'s shallop, a smaller boat used for cruising the shoreline. The men intended to inspect a large inlet that Robert Coffin had visited in the bay area years before. He claimed it was a promising site to build a town.

"I wish they'd take us with them," Danny said. He was growing tired of sitting around and doing nothing.

Just then Dr. Fuller strode up. "Danny, I've spoken to Mr. Bradford, and he's agreed to let you go with the shallop. Put on the warmest clothes you've got. It's going to be cold in that boat!"

"Can't I go too?" Dixie asked.

"No, lass. I want you to stay with Mrs. Bradford. Her husband has asked if I could spare you, and the poor woman is in a miserable condition."

Dixie agreed, although Danny knew she would much rather explore than stay on the ship. She helped Danny find as many warm clothes as he could possibly wear, then went to wave goodbye as he boarded the shallop with the men.

Besides Robert Coffin, the shallop contained several Saints—Edward and John Tilley, Bradford, Winslow, and Governor Carver with his servant John Howland. Captain Standish, Richard Warren, and Stephen Hopkins went along to represent the Strangers. The air was bitterly cold, and the salt spray cut like a knife as it whipped across the open boat. They spotted Indians on the beach, but as they climbed out of the small boat to make camp there for the night on the beach, the Indians slipped back into the woods.

Uncomfortable about the Indians' presence, the group posted sentries to keep watch. Danny was so exhausted he fell asleep at once, praying that he wouldn't freeze to death while he was sleeping. Early the next morning, Standish shook him roughly, shouting, "Attack! We're under attack!"

Danny heard strange cries that sounded like "Woach! Woach! Ha! Ha! Woach!" coming from the woods. Frightened, he grabbed his matchlock. He shot into the air, afraid of hitting someone, and several other men fired the weapons into the trees. Silence fell as their attackers seemed to withdraw. "After them!" Standish called out.

I'd just as soon not! Danny thought, but he had no choice. They followed Standish as well as they could for about a quarter of a mile, but the Indians were nowhere to be found. When they returned to their camp, daylight revealed arrows littering the ground. Fortunately, no one had been wounded.

Concerned about another attack, the men packed their gear and set out again in the shallop with Coffin at the tiller. But it began to snow, and the wind rose steadily. Danny was so miserable he could hardly think. *I almost wish I'd stayed on the ship!*

Sometime just before dark, they tried to run up more sail. With a snap, the mast broke into three pieces that plunged into the water. The sail went with them.

"Lord, be merciful unto us!" Coffin shouted. It was now too dark to do anything about their situation. Everyone rowed desperately, and at last they managed to land the shallop and build a fire. "A good thing we got a fire," Danny said, his teeth chattering. "We'd die in this weather without one."

"Aye, God has taken care of us," William Bradford nodded.

In the morning Coffin announced that they were on an island in the inlet they were seeking. The weather forced them to remain there for two days. Early on Monday morning, December 11, they sounded the natural harbor and found it was deep enough for ships to enter. Anxious to return to the ship to tell everyone about the site, Standish ordered Coffin to take the shallop straight across twenty-five miles of open water to the *Mayflower* rather than hug the coast. It was a dangerous move in a small boat at that time of year, but the storms stayed away.

The sun was shining brightly as they skimmed across the bay and tied up alongside the *Mayflower* that afternoon. The expedition had been gone a full week. Dixie dashed to Danny and hugged him, her relief at his return shining in her eyes.

"Oh, Danny! I was so scared I'd never see you again!" Dixie blurted as she hugged him a second time. For once Danny didn't mind the attention—it was good to be back with the others.

"Where's Dorothy?" Mr. Bradford had stepped on

deck and was looking for his wife.

"Poor Mr. Bradford," Dixie murmured. William Brewster walked up and took Bradford by the arm, steering him away from the rest of the group.

With tears in her eyes, Dixie whispered to Danny, "She . . . she fell overboard—Mrs. Bradford—and drowned." Danny could hardly believe his ears, but he knew it had to be true. Arriving in the New World had not made Mrs. Bradford better, and everyone knew it. Danny watched sadly as Brewster helped Bradford below deck.

"Fell overboard?" Danny repeated. "But how?"

"Nobody knows," Dixie answered, then added, "She lost her mind, Danny. She wasn't herself. We'll never know for sure what happened."

In the days that followed, Danny heard rumors that the young woman had committed suicide, but there was no proof. William Bradford was almost wild with grief; his friends crowded around to comfort him. "We've always leaned on him," Dr. Fuller said simply. "Now he is the one who needs help."

While they were away, two others had died—young Jasper More, one of John Carver's servants; and James Chilton, who left a wife and daughter to be cared for by the colony.

"A dozen others are flat in their bunks—too sick to move," the doctor said. "We're in the New World at last, but it seems as if our troubles are only beginning."

Most of the passengers wanted to land as soon as they heard about the new harbor, but Governor John Carver was anxious to let everyone have a say. They spent three more days debating before finally voting to settle in Plymouth, as they decided to call it. On December 15, the *Mayflower* weighed anchor and moved across the bay toward their new home.

But even after they arrived things moved slowly. A severe storm swept through, preventing them from working more than a few hours each day. The sick list grew longer, and many died. Danny and Dixie had never experienced so much death—it made them more desperate than ever to return home. It was so much easier to stay alive in twentieth-century America!

Danny helped John Alden dig the new graves. Alden stood looking at the hole in the ground, his face grim. "I'm thinking these graves will not be the last. It's a long time until spring. Too long, I'm thinking."

"We'll make it, John," Danny reassured him, knowing John, at least, would live through the winter.

"We've got no help but our own hands," Alden returned.

Danny shook his head. "That's not true. We have God on our side."

The muscular young man looked at Danny for a moment, then nodded. "You've become one of the Saints, Danny Fortune, talking like that."

Danny was embarrassed but managed to smile. "I don't know about that, John. What about you?" He knew that John Alden had never been very religious.

John took a moment to answer. "Been thinking quite a lot about that. I've decided it's better to be a Saint than a Stranger. There's something special about the way they see things, and I want God with me. You think Mr. Bradford and the rest will have me?"

"I think God will have you," Danny said warmly. "And that's good enough, right?"

John Alden straightened his back, looked up at the sky, and said briefly, "Aye, that's good enough, Danny!"

11

ON CHRISTMAS DAY WORK ACTUALLY began on the new settlement. The Pilgrims did not take the day off—the Saints didn't believe in celebrating Christmas or Easter or any other traditional holidays. Because many of the men were too sick to work, the younger boys like Danny were allowed to go ashore and join the work parties.

Early that morning, Dixie helped cook breakfast for the men. Afterward, John Billington cornered her, saying, "Well, now, Dixie, I'll have a kiss from my sweetheart before I go to work."

Danny stood nearby, partially hidden in the shadows. He held back for a moment to see how his sister would react. Dixie tried to dodge under John's arm, but he caught her and laughed at her efforts to escape. "You sure are a feisty one, Dixie!"

Just at that moment Danny stepped out of his hiding place and grabbed Billington's arm. "Let her go, John!" he demanded.

John was much larger and stronger than Danny. He drew back his arm and hit Danny square in the mouth, driving him back against the bulkhead. "Danny!" Dixie screamed and threw herself between the two.

"That's right, Danny—go ahead and hide behind a girl's skirts," John snorted, then left them.

"Your mouth is swollen," Dixie said. "What a bully he is—just like his father!"

Danny reached up to touch his aching mouth. At least it wasn't bleeding. "I guess John inherited his dad's nasty temper. He'll get over it."

Normally Danny would have been right about John, but things did not go well for the young Billington the rest of that day. He went into the Great Cabin, where many of the personal weapons were stored, to get his father's flintlock. Most of the settlement's gunpowder was also temporarily stored there to keep it dry.

Danny had asked Captain Standish if he could take a weapon to hunt with, and the soldier had agreed. But when Danny entered the cabin, he discovered John there, picking up his father's gun. There was a strained silence, and John sneered, "I'm surprised that Standish will let you go with the men. You ought to put on a dress and stay with the women!"

Danny said carefully, "John, we don't need any more trouble than we've got. Let's forget it. I want to be friends."

But John laughed and picked up the flintlock. As he primed it, standing dangerously close to the open barrel of gunpowder, he said, "Just stay away from me, that's all."

Danny stared at him. Had John lost his mind? "John," he began nervously, "you really shouldn't prime that weapon in here. Just one spark and the gunpowder will blow us all up—the ship too."

"Don't try to tell me about how to use a weapon!" John snapped, swinging the flintlock up and pulling the trigger. The musket emitted a tremendous flash from the powder in the firing pan. At that exact moment, Miles

Standish walked through the door.

His face turned pale, and he leaped forward. "You stupid boy!" he shouted, ripping the musket from John. Furious, Standish threw him a punch that drove the boy backward. "Are you such a fool as to prime a musket while standing over a barrel of gunpowder?" He lashed John with his tongue until the boy was pale as paper. Finally he said, "I'll not see a musket in your clumsy hands again, you hear me? Now get back on the boat!"

As John stumbled out the door, Danny said, "Do you really mean you won't let John use a musket again?"

"As long as we aren't desperate for an extra shot, yes. We can't afford to let anyone take foolhardy risks." Standish still looked angry. "Now, let's forget about hunting for a while and get to work!"

They joined a work crew and began chopping down pine trees and sawing them into planks for the construction of the community's first dwelling, the Common House. The building was to be only twenty feet square. It would serve as a shelter for the workers who were left on shore each night to guard the settlement's precious tools. Danny had expected they would be living in log cabins, but when he asked he discovered no one even knew what a log cabin was.

By the time the sun went down, Danny's arms felt as though they were about to drop off. He staggered weakly to his bed on ship after eating supper. *If we ever get home, I'll never complain about having to help around the house again,* he promised himself as he collapsed onto his bed. *These people do more work in a week than I've done in my whole life!*

The next day Danny was put to work again. The leaders were laying out the measurements for New England's first main street. It was to run uphill with two rows of houses on either side. A fort would be built at the top of the hill.

They worked on in the rain and the cold—the small houses were not easy to build. First, they had to lay a foundation of stone, then erect an open frame on top. They cut their own trees, trimmed to roughly square sections with a broadax. For walls, two-inch planks had to be stripped of their bark and sawed. The joints and cracks in the walls were filled with clay. There was no glass, so oilpaper was used in the windows. Fieldstone was used for fireplaces and chimneys. For roofs they used thatch, as generations of people had done in England. Unfortunately, gathering thatch at Plymouth meant miles of tramping through the meadows and along the creek banks. There was the constant possibility of being cut off from the settlement by a surprise Indian attack.

As the town took shape, more and more people became sick—no one was sure why. Everyone had begun to call the illness the General Sickness. On January 1, Digory Priest died, and a week later, Christopher Martin followed. Many others were unable to work, and the healthy people had to spend precious time caring for the sick.

Danny's hands grew callus, but he didn't get sick.

"What would you do if I died, Dixie?" he asked her one evening after hearing the news of yet another death.

Dixie whirled around to face him. "Don't even *say* things like that! We've got to stay well and find the Recall Unit so we can go home."

"I'm sorry, Dixie," Danny apologized. "I didn't mean to upset you. It's just that so many people have gotten sick and died."

Dixie nodded, then said, "Danny, I . . . I've been doing something you may think is wrong."

He glanced at her sharply. "What?" he demanded.

"Well, it's not only the passengers who are sick," she said. "Several of the crew are down as well—and they don't care anything about each other! When one of them gets sick, the others don't even *try* to help.

"Anyway, a few days ago, I found out that Edward Hill—the crewman who was such a friend to William Butten—was sick. I took him some food, and he was so surprised! Well, I started taking care of him—and some others too."

"So? What's wrong with that?"

Dixie bit her lip, then added carefully, "Well—there's a little more to it. Edward went to sleep once while I was there. His little bag of personal things was right next to him. I got to wondering if he could have been the one who took the Recall Unit—so I looked in the bag."

"Was it there?"

"No," she admitted. "But I didn't really think it would be. I realized then that I had a good excuse to be in the crew's quarters. Most of them are up on deck during the daytime, so I started taking a peek into some of their stuff."

"Dixie!" Danny exclaimed. "If you get caught, everyone will think you're a thief!"

"I know—and it scares me to death!" she returned quickly. "But we've got to do *something*! We can't stay here forever."

"I guess so," Danny admitted slowly. "But be careful.

It's a long shot that you'll run across it digging through the crew's things."

January wore on, and the General Sickness struck down William Bradford. Dixie took him his meals, wishing his wife were still alive to help take care of him.

On Sunday, January 14, the Common House was finished. The group celebrated with the usual prayer and Scripture reading. It was comforting to peer down on the solid-looking walls and thick thatched roof from the ship. The new building gave the wild shore at least a hint of civilization.

But at six o'clock that night, a panicked cry of alarm ran through the *Mayflower*. "The Common House is on fire!"

At first everyone thought it was an Indian attack, and the men rushed for their muskets. They stormed up ladders and over the side into the shallop, but the tide was too low to land. The rescue crew had to sit in the boat for an agonizing three-quarters of an hour as the smoke billowed up on shore. Many wondered out loud if there would be anyone alive to save once they finally got there.

When they arrived, they found everyone who had remained on land busy fighting the fire. It was caused not by Indians, but by a spark that flew up from the fireplace into the thatch. Fortunately they snuffed it out before any of the beams caught fire, so the roof was saved.

William Bradford had been lying sick in the Common House during the fire, unable to move. Half-open barrels of gunpowder and charged muskets shared the building with him. If it had not been for a few brave and quick-thinking men who dragged the weapons outside at the first hint of fire, it would have been all over for him.

The next week, Rose Standish, the quiet wife of Captain Miles Standish, died, bringing the total dead in January to eight—and the General Sickness was only beginning!

Dozens of those who did not have the General Sickness had been suffering from colds and scurvy. Scurvy in particular was an extremely dangerous disease, Danny learned. Often, a victim would feel well and try to go back to work before he was ready. The crew had seen more than one man step from his hammock announcing he was fine, walk a few feet, and drop dead.

Now in the worst of winter, another terrible virus swept through the weakened colony. William Bradford, Governor Carver, Edward Winslow, William White, William Mullins, and Stephen Hopkins all came down with it. They were so weak they were unable to perform the simplest physical tasks.

The weather grew worse, and the driving rain melted away most of the clay they had used to patch their houses—exposing them even more to the frigid, damp air and bitter winds. The storm was so fierce that even the *Mayflower* was thought to be in danger of breaking apart in the harbor.

The death toll climbed—William White, William Mullins, and Isaac Allerton's wife, Mary, passed away. Dr. Samuel Fuller did what he could to ease their suffering, but his old-fashioned medicine offered little help. It was an awful time—so bad that some people might have given up, left the sick to their doom in the wilderness, and sailed for home.

But that did not happen. Instead, those who were well worked for the sick without complaining. They fetched wood, built fires, cooked, made beds, washed infected clothes, dressed and undressed the sick—all without any concern for their own health.

Danny and Dixie did their part to help the sick. In the middle of February, John Billington Jr. and his father and younger brother, Francis, came down with the virus.

"What do *you* want?" John said weakly when he saw Danny standing beside his bunk. The sick boy was wrapped in a dirty blanket.

"I thought you might like some soup, John," Danny said with a smile. "It's pretty good. Dixie made it just for you."

"Don't want none of your food. Just leave me alone," Billington grumbled. But Danny refused to argue. He sat down, pulled the older boy up into a sitting position, and made him eat. Every day after that Danny returned, trying his best to be patient and friendly. However hard it was to get along with John, Danny did not like seeing him sick.

But John got worse, not better. Finally Danny and Dr. Fuller pulled him out of his filthy clothes and reeking blanket and took them to the river to wash them.

"You'll feel better once you're all cleaned up," Danny promised when he brought them back. After John had been washed and dressed, Danny got up to leave. "Well, you're all clean now. I'll check in on you tomorrow and see how you're doing," he announced.

"Wait a minute," John said. There was an odd look on his pale face. "I . . . I reckon I got to say something to you, Danny."

"What's that?"

"I was wrong to try to kiss Dixie—and I was wrong to hit you." It was obvious that John was not used to apologizing, but he did his best.

He struggled to continue, but Danny said, "Don't worry about it, John. Let's just forget it. You might say something to Dixie, but she's not angry with you. I'm sure you'll be out of this bunk pretty soon and back to work."

John relaxed and tried again. "I never thought I'd see so much death, Danny. It gives a person a fear, don't it? Makes you think about what all the ministers say." He shrugged and said, "I never thought about dying much, but I've thought about it lately." He gave an embarrassed look and asked, "Danny, would you . . . say a prayer for me?"

Danny stared at him. This was the last thing he had expected! Then he said slowly, "Sure. But you should pray for yourself too, you know. Just tell the Lord you're sorry for all the wrong you've done." Then he added, "And if you ask Him to save you, I know He will."

Finally John said, "I . . . I ain't been very good, I'm afraid."

"Well, the Bible says that Jesus is a friend to sinners—I'm sure that means He's your friend too, John!" Danny saw John's eyes grow hopeful and continued, "Look, I'll start praying, and you just jump in and tell God you want to be forgiven. He'll do it!"

So the two prayed. When they finished, Danny looked up to see tears in John's eyes. "I . . . I think it worked!" John whispered excitedly. "I feel cleaned out!"

They talked for a short time, then Danny went to tell Dixie what had happened. "Stop by to visit him, will you, Dixie? He needs all the help he can get right now."

"Of course, Danny." She nodded, then said, "Isn't it funny how things have worked out? If John hadn't gotten sick, he'd still hate us both. Now he's a Christian."

"Well, seventeen people have died this month," Danny said seriously. "I guess nobody can live through that and not be changed. It's like when Mr. Mullins died. Even though he was a Stranger, he chose two Saints to take care of his property back in England. I guess that couldn't have happened before this."

The month of February finally passed, and March began on a hopeful note as the warm winds came and the sun came out. Yet the optimism did not last long.

John Billington Sr., stubborn even in the face of the crisis that had killed so many of the Strangers and half the settlement, refused to obey Miles Standish's orders to stand watch. He was arrested, tried, and found guilty. Carver ordered him punished by having his neck and heels tied together—a typical punishment for the time. Billington's face fell, and he begged and pleaded until Governor Carver at last changed his sentence.

But something even more startling happened on March 10. The settlers were constantly on their guard against Indians, so they were shocked to see a tall, handsome Indian wearing nothing but a fringe of leather around his waist come striding into the camp that morning. They all stared as he laid his hand on his chest and said, "You ale have? Samoset, me. I like ale."

Standish said instantly, "It's a trap!" But he was over-ruled, and the Indian talked with the leaders late into the night. He told them he had learned their language sailing with English captains along the northern coast. He also told them that a powerful chief called Massasoit lived only forty miles away.

The next morning Samoset left, but he returned the next day with four other Indians who had beaver skins to trade. "This could be very profitable!" Edward Winslow exclaimed. "Beaver skins bring a good price in England. We might be able to make a decent living trading."

Things moved quickly, and in four days Samoset brought another Indian to the camp. His name was Squanto, and he spoke much better English than Samoset. He was the last surviving member of the Pawtuxet tribe that had lived at Plymouth.

As March rolled on, Squanto proved to be an important friend to the Pilgrims—so much so that William Bradford called him "a special instrument of God."

"Here we've been worried about the Indians killing us," Danny commented to Captain Standish one day, "and it looks like they're going to be good friends."

Standish shook his head. "I doubt they're all that friendly. We'll have to kill a few of them in time, I'm sure."

Danny shook his head. "Why? This is their land, isn't it?"

Standish stared at him, perplexed. "Danny, that's the way countries grow! There wouldn't be an England if some of our people hadn't fought to take it away from whoever was there."

"I still don't think it's right," Danny said. He thought

of the few reservations of Indians around his home state, and he felt sad. *If only things could turn out differently!*

Edward Winslow had been listening, and he walked up and gave Danny a pat on the shoulder. "You have a good, kind heart, Danny—maybe someday we'll be able to live as friends with the Indians. But for now, we need to do what we have to to survive."

Danny looked toward the dark woods to their west. "I know what you're saying," he said quietly, "but I still feel sorry for the Indians." He left the two men and went to find his sister.

12

"I DON'T KNOW WHAT we'd have done without Squanto!" John Alden said more than once during the month of April. He echoed the feelings of all the colonists.

The Pawtuxet had showed them how helpful he could be to their survival when he said one day, "I go to fish for eels."

Danny and Dixie said instantly, "Can we go?" Constance was with them and automatically included herself in the request.

Squanto nodded, and the three followed him down to a nearby river at low tide. "We don't have any fishing poles, Squanto," Dixie protested. "How can we catch any fish?"

"Take off shoes," he said, and when they were barefoot he walked out on the muddy banks of the little stream. He began to move up and down so his feet worked deep into the mud. Suddenly he reached down and grabbed something. Straightening, he tossed it toward them. It was a slithering eel a foot long—and it hit Constance right in the face!

She screamed and backed up, her feet slipping. She landed flat in the mud. Danny and Dixie burst out laughing—Constance always looked so nice, it was funny to see her plastered with mud. Her face red, she jerked herself up. "You wouldn't think it was so funny if it happened to you!" she cried. "I'm going home!"

Danny ran after her, trying to persuade her to stay, but she was thoroughly disgusted with him. "No!" she shouted. "I've tried to be sweethearts with you, Danny Fortune—but no more! There are lots of others who like me well enough!"

Danny went back to where Dixie was standing. "I guess that was 'Goodbye, Danny,' huh?" she asked.

"Sure was," he said. "It's probably better this way. She's too forward for a girl."

"She's too forward for a *boy*!" Dixie said. "Her father's awful servants have both been after her. If her dad knew it, he'd have a fit!"

"I don't think he cares much, Dixie." Danny shrugged. "Well, we told Squanto we wanted to catch some eels—we better get to work!"

By the end of the afternoon, Squanto had taught them how to catch the squirming eels. When they got back to town they were praised for their skill—the eels tasted much better than either of the twins had hoped.

Later Squanto showed them how to plant corn, four kernels to the hill, in true Indian fashion. He warned them that unless they fertilized the ground with fish, the whole crop would come to nothing.

"Fish!" Governor Carver groaned. "We can't even catch enough fish to eat for ourselves!"

"I show you." Squanto assured them that in the middle of April the Town Brook would be swarming with fish coming to spawn. The fish arrived exactly on schedule and were easily caught under his expert direction. He then showed them how to bury the fish into the ground, three to each hill, with the fish heads close to the kernels. Squanto also warned them that unless they set a guard until the fish were rotten, the wolves would dig them up and eat them. The colonists readily accepted his advice.

It was during April that the *Mayflower* finally set sail for England. Captain Jones had left ten of his best crewmen in the shallow graves on the hill, but he could wait no longer. He had learned to appreciate the men and women of Plymouth as much as they did him.

"We're really alone now," Dixie said as the ship slipped over the horizon. "And no closer to going home than ever. What if the Recall Unit is on the *Mayflower*, Danny? We might be here from now on!"

Danny had to agree. "It sure looks that way." He managed a smile and said, "Well, if it is, there's nothing we can do about it. Let's try to make the best of it, Dixie."

And so they did, all summer long.

Many things happened that summer. Good old Governor Carver died, and William Bradford was elected in his place. William White's widow, Susanna, married Edward Winslow, whose wife had died from the General Sickness. John Alden and Priscilla Mullins fell in love and were planning to be married.

But it was Constance Hopkins who provided everyone with the most drama. After giving up on Danny, she began to flirt with her father's two servants, Edward Doten and Edward Leister. The two had been among the chief instigators of the mutiny before the *Mayflower Compact* was signed. Soon they were competing ferociously for a kind word or a smile from her. Constance encouraged the rivalry—she loved being the center of attention.

At dawn on June 18, Doten and Leister seized their swords and daggers and went to a deserted stretch of the beach. There, sword in one hand, dagger in the other, they began Plymouth's first duel. Snarling and cursing, the pair raged up and down the shore. Doten sank his rapier deep into Leister's thigh, and was slashed in return with Leister's dagger. Ignoring the blood, they cut and slashed at each other with all their strength.

Their battle cries and clashing swords woke the colony. Miles Standish came charging in, furious. He disarmed them and marched them to face Governor William Bradford, who was every bit as angry as the captain.

"I'll not put up with this!" Bradford said angrily. "Tie them together head and heels. Let that cool their hot blood!" The men were tied up, but Bradford was not finished. "Bring Constance here!" he commanded.

Standish brought Constance out in front of everyone, where Bradford gave her a sizzling lecture and ordered her father to give her a thrashing. Danny was never sure whether Stephen Hopkins carried out the governor's orders.

The summer continued, and John Billington Jr. was captured by Indians. Fortunately for him, he was returned unharmed. For days later, he swaggered around the camp, rather proud of himself over the incident.

The threat of hostile Indian attack was always there, especially from the Wampanoag Indians, who were reportedly warlike. As the summer faded, William Bradford decided to take action.

"The sensible thing to do is to send ambassadors to

them—find out their intentions." He chose ten men, put Miles Standish in charge, and sent Squanto and two other Indians in the shallop. They reached the harbor near the Wampanong Camp late the following day, September 19. There they obtained guides who took them across the bay to the camp of Chief Massasoit. The group soon discovered that the Wampanoags were far more afraid of *them* than the other way around. It was easy to persuade them to come to Plymouth for a peaceful feast.

When they returned, Bradford said, "On the third of October in Leyden, there is always a Thanksgiving celebration. I believe we should have the same here."

Preparations for the first official American Thanksgiving Day were soon under way. A messenger was sent to Massasoit to invite him, and Bradford sent four men out hunting. In one day they killed enough wild turkeys to feed the whole company for almost a week.

Chief Massasoit arrived as hoped—with no less than ninety hungry men—and pouches fat with popping corn.

But when the chief arrived and saw the preparations, he apparently realized there would not be enough food. He sent some of his hunters into the woods. Soon they returned with five deer.

Danny said, "This is really something to be at the most famous Thanksgiving! I haven't seen so much food in a long time."

The celebration lasted for three days. Between meals the men held shooting exhibitions with guns and bows. Massasoit was impressed to learn that Miles Standish could handle a bow and arrow almost as well as an Indian. And in the wrestling matches, John Alden put every man, Pilgrim or Indian, flat on his back.

Danny sat a little ways from the happy crowd and took in the view with Dixie. The maples had turned gold and the oak leaves reddish brown. Flashes of scarlet lit the marshes, and the waters of the harbor shone a crystal blue. The rows of new thatched houses stood ready for winter.

Governor Bradford rose and made a brief speech before the final meal, and then he prayed to thank God for His goodness. As he prayed, Danny's mind flitted to the graves in the cemetery and the suffering of the past year. No matter how difficult the year had been, the Saints had never doubted God's goodness. Danny wished he could be more like them.

"Look, Danny," Dixie whispered when the meal was over. "John's coming this way."

Danny turned and saw John Billington picking his way through the crowd. "Hey, John," he called out.

"Hello, Danny," he said. Then he looked at Dixie. "Hello, Dixie."

"Did you get plenty to eat?" she asked with a smile.

"Oh, more than enough!" he answered. "I . . . I want to say something to you, Danny," he glanced quickly at Dixie. "Alone, if possible."

"I'll move along," Dixie offered.

"No, wait," he said quickly, then hesitated. He seemed to be struggling with some sort of problem. "You can stay."

The twins looked at him expectantly, waiting for him to go on.

"It's been a good year, hasn't it?" John began at last.

"A hard year," Danny nodded, wondering where John

was heading with this. "But a good one. I've sure learned a lot!"

"Me too!" John said eagerly. "And that's what I want to tell you two." He shifted his feet uneasily, then blurted, "Do you remember when I was sick, Danny—and you prayed with me?"

"Sure!"

"Well, I've never forgotten that," John said. "I won't say it's been easy trying to be a Christian. I don't claim to be a saint—not like Mr. Bradford or Elder Brewster."

"There aren't many like that, John," Dixie said. "But you're doing well. I've noticed."

"Have you really?" he brightened at her words. "It's not easy—especially not with my family. They don't hold much with religion. Matter of fact, I tried to tell my father how I'd prayed and asked God to help me—but he just laughed." His face fell, and he lifted his eyes to look directly into Danny's.

"The thing is," he said, "ever since that day you prayed, I've tried to live better—but there was always one thing. . . . I've done a lot of wrong things, and after I prayed it was as if they all were gone—but not this."

"Was it something you did to me?" Danny asked. "I don't remember anything like that."

"Don't suppose you ever knew about it," John said. Then he asked suddenly, "Do you remember the day you came on the *Mayflower* for the first time?"

A shiver ran up Danny's spine. "I sure do, John!"

"Well, I was looking for you below deck . . . and I found you," John said. "But you were asleep." He looked down at the ground. "I saw a string around your neck and figured it was some kind of a locket. So I cut it with my knife and slipped it off, and"—he slowly reached into his pocket—"well, here it is."

Danny could hardly believe his eyes as John hauled the silver Recall Unit out of his pocket. "I wanted to give it back, but it was so unusual. . . ." John confessed as he handed it over. "Anyway, I took it, and I'm sorry. Will you be able to overlook it?"

"Of course!" Danny cried. He slapped John on the back and said, "If I ever had any doubt about whether you'd become a Christian, it's gone now, John Billington!"

Dixie threw her arms around John's neck and kissed him on the cheek. He turned bright red and mumbled, "I'm glad *that's* over! Now maybe I can get some sleep again!"

Danny held up the silver disc as John turned and left. It glittered in his trembling hand as the sunlight struck it. "Thank you, God!" he whispered in a shaky voice.

"It's a miracle," Dixie said, her face lit up with excitement. "We can go home now!"

"*If* it works," Danny agreed. "It's been a long time, Dixie. Zacharias has probably forgotten about us, or at least given up on us. Who knows? The Chrono-Shuttle may have broken down."

"I doubt it!" Dixie replied. "I think it's time for us to go."

"Well, we can't go right *now*," Danny argued. "I mean, we can't just disappear in front of them all. As a matter of fact," he said slowly, "how in the world are we going to do it?"

"Why, just push the button!"

"No, that's not what I mean. What will they think when we disappear—all our friends? What would *you* think if one of the Saints just vanished? Wouldn't you be worried?"

Dixie nodded slowly. "I see what you mean." She thought hard for a moment, then said, "Well, we'll think of something."

"Sure—as smart as I am," Danny managed to keep a straight face, "it won't take long!"

But Danny was mistaken. The more they thought about ways of leaving without creating an uproar, the more difficult it became. Days passed, and no solutions came to either of them.

"Where's that *smart* brother of mine?" Dixie asked in exasperation several weeks later. "I thought you were going to find a way to sneak us out of here."

"I've thought of a thousand options," Danny groaned. "And they all have one thing in common— none of them will work! I guess we're just going to have to leave any way we can!"

That same afternoon, a lookout came running up the streets of the village. "A ship! A ship from home!" he yelled, and soon every person who could walk lined the shore to stare at the sails.

"She's English!" Miles Standish reported when he saw the red-and-white cross of St. George.

The ship lowered its boats, and soon Governor Bradford was eagerly greeting the newcomers. William Brewster and his wife embraced their twenty-year-old son, and Edward Winslow greeted his two brothers John and Kenelm. Altogether there were thirty-five passengers, most of them with welcome skills.

The people of Plymouth were delighted by the arrival, but no one more than Danny. He was practically jumping up and down with joy.

"What's wrong with you?" Dixie demanded.

"Nothing! Absolutely nothing!" he shouted. "But there's our ticket home!" He pointed at the ship—the name *Fortune* was painted on the side. "What could be more perfect! She'll leave in a few days—and we'll be on her."

"Oh, I get it! We can slip away any time that way, can't we? And no one here will worry!"

They quickly discovered that the *Fortune* would leave in less than a week. Danny went to Dr. Fuller at once. "Doctor, I'm afraid I haven't been completely honest with you. I hope you'll forgive me."

Fuller gave him a hard look. "What's the trouble, my boy? I'll do what I can to help you."

"Oh, you've already done that, sir!" Danny protested. "Dixie and I were in desperate trouble back in England. You were the only one who would help us, so we became your indentured servants.

"You see, Dixie and I, we'd like to go back home. I want to pay you what we owe you for our passage and the remaining time we would have spent working as your servants."

Danny held out the gold coins his great-uncles had given him. Fuller stared at them. "Why—I am dumbfounded, Danny! Why didn't you tell me you had money? But what will you do? Do you have any family?"

"Yes, sir, and we're going back to them as soon as we can get there!"

"Ah!" Fuller nodded wisely. "I said to myself the first time I saw you, 'Those two are runaways.' And I was right!" He chuckled and shook his head. "Hard to fool a wise old owl such as myself!" he exclaimed proudly.

"It certainly is!" Danny nodded, hiding a smile. "But we want you to have the money. It's only right."

"I'll take the fare, but no more. You've earned your way." He put his arm around Danny and added, "I'll miss you, lad. All of us will miss the two of you!"

"And we'll miss you too, Dr. Fuller!" Danny said. "It's been a wonderful year. I'll never forget it!"

Word about their coming departure traveled quickly. Danny and Dixie had to explain over and over again how they had left their home and family under disagreeable circumstances and had to get back. Many tried to persuade them to stay, but Governor Bradford said, "We shall all miss you, but it's right for you to go home to your family."

Three days later, they went down to the harbor for the last time. Everyone in Plymouth was there—the departure of the *Fortune* was quite an event in the life of the little town.

Danny and Dixie said goodbye to everyone. It was hard to believe they would never see their friends again. As the sails of the *Fortune* filled and the ship slowly moved away, tears began to run down Dixie's cheeks. Danny wiped his eyes and said in a husky voice, "Goodbye, Saints! Goodbye, Strangers!" As the land slowly sank into the sea, the twins searched out a secluded corner of the ship.

It was a bright day, but very cold. It had been more than a year since they had left Zacharias and Mordecai's quirky basement lab. Finally they reached a deserted spot in the lower regions of the ship. "Well, I guess this is as good a spot as any."

"I'm scared all over again!" Dixie said. "What if it doesn't work?"

Danny clamped his jaw firmly shut and pulled the Recall Unit from beneath his shirt. "It *has* to work. Hold my hand, Dixie. We're going back home!"

They held hands, and Danny took one last look around. *Goodbye, 1621,* he thought, then jabbed the exposed *return* button in the center of the unit.

Instantly the earth seemed to quake. "It's working, Dixie!" Danny shouted.

They were swaying, and the space around them was suddenly enveloped in a mist of green fog. The hard boards of the floor seemed to turn into Jell-O, and a low hum began. The hum escalated into a high pitch—so intense Danny almost screamed. Without warning, they were rocked by a huge jolt. Abruptly, the humming stopped.

Danny opened his eyes and saw Zacharias' beady black eyes peering through the glass of the Chrono-Shuttle. He let go of Dixie's hand and yelled, "We're home! Dixie, we're home!"

The twins stood up and tumbled over each other in their race to escape the machine.

13

"WHAT ARE YOU TWO DOING back so soon?" Zacharias demanded impatiently. Mordecai stood behind him, the same suspicious look echoed on his face.

Danny stared at the little men in absolute shock. "So *soon!*" he yelped angrily. "What are you talking about? We've been gone for over a year!"

Mordecai shook his head in disgust. "You must have hit your head on something while you were gone! You're crazy!"

Dixie jumped in. "Crazy! You're the ones who are crazy!" She shook her finger under their noses and added, "Is *this* all the thanks we get for risking our lives in your silly machine?"

Suddenly Zacharias's face changed. He studied the twins' faces, then whirled and dashed back to a huge bank of buttons and digital readouts on the far side of the room. Mordecai followed him, his eyes following his brother's every move. They heard Zacharias mumbling to himself as he rapidly pulled switches and pushed buttons, all the while making notes in a tiny book. Finally he said, "A-ha!" and came rushing to stand in front of Danny and Dixie.

"How long did you stay in the year 1620?" Zacharias asked.

"We got there on September 4. We sailed on the *May-*

flower and stayed in Plymouth. Then we hopped on a ship and used the Recall Unit on November 3, 1621."

The odd little scientist bobbed his head up and down while Danny spoke. A small smile twisted the corners of his lips upward. "Well, that is all very interesting—*very* interesting indeed! I know Brother Mordecai will want extensive reports from you."

"I certainly will!" Mordecai scurried around to get closer to them and asked, "Exactly how did the Pilgrims—"

"Just one moment!" Zacharias broke in. "There will be plenty of time to do your research. But before we go on, you kids need to know something." He frowned and shook his head. "I don't completely understand it, but the time you spent in the past didn't take up the same amount of time here."

"What exactly do you mean?" Danny demanded.

"Look at the date on the Chrono-Shuttle control panel," Zacharias instructed.

Danny and Dixie both turned and went to look. The indicator display marked *Present* displayed the date and time in blazing red numbers.

"B-but—that says it's only April 14! The same day and year we left!" Danny stuttered. "That *can't* be right!"

"I suspect it is right," Zacharias disagreed. "Einstein theorized that the faster you move, the more time changes. Say a spaceship leaves the earth for other galaxies. Naturally, its speed will be very great. As a result, the people on the ship will not age nearly so much as those left on the earth. If a trip lasts a thousand years of earth time, for example, the astronauts will hardly age at all—maybe only a few weeks. But when they return, everyone they know back home will be long dead."

"That's horrible!" Dixie cried. "I wouldn't want to go!"

"That's because you don't have a scientific spirit," Zacharias sniffed. "Now *I* would go in an instant!"

"Sure you would!" Danny snorted. "You're too scared to travel in your own time machine."

Zacharias's face reddened. He started to argue, but Dixie said, "Oh, can't this wait! I don't want to argue with you right now—I want to go home."

"So do I!" Danny agreed. "Our trip may have lasted only a few hours here, but I haven't seen my mother or little brother in over a year."

"Wait a minute!" Mordecai shouted. "You can't leave *now*! I want to hear about everything. Goodness knows we've paid for it."

"We'll come back for that," Dixie promised. "For now, take us home."

"Very well," Zacharias relented. "We'll take you, but you must return very soon. Tomorrow would be best. After all, you owe us."

Danny stared at him in unbelief. "We *owe* you?" he asked. "We took your little trip—we risked our lives for you. You know the machine works. What more could you want?"

"We've taken care of our end," Mordecai noted stiffly. "Giving us a report was part of the bargain."

"Oh, come on, Danny!" Dixie said. "We'll come back. It's only fair."

"I'm glad to see *one* of you has some sense of fairness and responsibility!" Zacharias said pointedly. He led them to the car, and all the way back to town, Mordecai pumped them for information.

He was absolutely convinced that the Pilgrims were

money-hungry frauds. "Now tell me the truth. They traveled to the New World for financial gain, right?"

"Are you sure you want the *truth*?" Dixie asked. "Or do you just want to prove what you already have decided to believe?"

"I am a historian!" Mordecai reminded them proudly. "I want *facts* not fables!"

"All right," Dixie said, "I'll give you a few facts!" For the rest of the trip she told him how the Pilgrims had risked their property and their lives for a cause they believed in. She told him how they had shared what little they had, and how they had served the sick unselfishly during the General Sickness. On and on she went as they drove down the highway.

By the time they pulled up in front of the Fortunes' apartment building, Mordecai was silent. As the twins stepped out of the car, he said, "I'll have to think of all you've told me. It . . . it wipes out all my theories!"

Dixie put her hand on his arm. "Don't worry, Mordecai. You're going to learn a lot of things and be a famous historian. But this is your first lesson—truth is more important than theory!"

She went over to stand with Danny in front of the old apartment building. They regarded it silently. "It looks pretty good, doesn't it, Dixie?"

"A lot better than the little houses in Plymouth!" she answered. "You know, I don't think I'll take things for granted so much. Things like hot water—and a warm room."

"Me either." They entered the building, made their way up the creaking steps, and stopped in front of the door.

"I feel funny!" Dixie said. "Almost sick to my stomach. Why is that?"

"Don't know—but I feel the same way. Look," Danny said, "*we* feel different, but Mom and Jimmy—why, they saw us just six hours ago! So let's act as normal as possible, okay?"

"Okay." Dixie smiled up at him, then tapped on the door.

It opened almost immediately. Their mother stood there, looking tired but happy. "Oh, you're back so soon!" she smiled. "I've just returned from the Terrys'."

Danny coughed loudly to hide the laugh that came to his throat and happily threw his arms around his mother. "Mom! We're so glad to see you!"

Ellen Fortune seemed caught off guard by the sudden embrace. She squeezed back, then said, "Well! I must say it's good to be gone from you two for a few hours if this is the hello I get," she said as they finally let her go. "I haven't had a hug like that in a *long* time!"

Jimmy came in, his eyes shining. Danny picked him up and whirled him around the room until he shrieked with happiness. Then Dixie had to have her turn hugging and tickling him. At last they all quieted down, and Mrs. Fortune said, "I've got spaghetti cooking. We can eat any time."

"Spaghetti my foot!" Danny shouted. "No noodles tonight! We're going out to celebrate. Come on, Mom, get your coat!"

"But, Danny, it's 9:30 at night—and we can't afford . . ." Their mother began to protest.

"Don't worry about it, Mom," Danny reassured her. "Money's on the way—just let us explain it to you at the restaurant."

They bundled Jimmy into a coat—he always was chilled at restaurants—and in less than thirty minutes they were sitting down at the Waterview Steak and Seafood House. They'd eaten there once years earlier but had not been able to afford it since then.

"Bring us four filet mignons," Danny ordered grandly, "with all the trimmings!"

The waiter left, eyeing their casual clothing with raised eyebrows.

"So tell me how you got this money," Mrs. Fortune began. "You haven't done anything wrong, I hope." She gave Dixie a quick glance. Dixie blushed, obviously recalling her shoplifting incident, and looked at Danny.

"Well, Mom—you remember Dad's uncles—Zacharias and Mordecai?" Danny began.

"Yes . . . but—"

Danny jumped in before she could finish. "Dixie and I went out to see them today. They aren't as strange and awful as you thought."

"I thought you said you were going to the library," his mother said, her eyes questioning.

Danny blushed. "We did. I'm sorry I lied to you. I know it's no excuse, but I didn't think you'd let us go to see them if you knew the truth."

"I wouldn't have," Mrs. Fortune said grimly. "They don't seem like good people—they sure didn't treat your father well. And they haven't done anything to help us since he disappeared!"

"Well, they've had a change of heart," Danny said. "Isn't that right, Dixie?"

"Oh, completely!" Dixie said. "In fact, they've agreed to help us."

"Help us? How?"

"Why, with money for one thing," Danny began. "They *insisted* on that part, didn't they, Dixie?"

"Wouldn't have it any other way!" she agreed. "In fact, as soon as the mail comes tomorrow," she waved a hand dramatically, "you're going to get quite a surprise!"

"A surprise?" Ellen Fortune looked confused.

"Would a certified check for *ten thousand dollars* surprise you a little bit, Mom?" Danny asked, watching his mother's face intently.

She looked stunned. "You've got to be joking." Mrs. Fortune studied her older children seriously.

At once Dixie said, "It's like this—we told them what a hard time we were having and how we needed money to help Jimmy and hire a detective to find Dad. When they heard about it, they said they'd give us the money— *if* we helped them in their laboratory occasionally."

"But—*ten thousand dollars!*" Their mother's face was pale and her hands were trembling. "That's a lot of money! What sort of work could you do that would be worth that much?"

"Oh, I think they just want to help us," Danny said quickly, winking at Dixie. "The work is just an excuse they thought up to make it look less like charity."

It took the entire meal to convince their mother the money was real. When they got ready to leave, Danny said, "Leave a twenty-dollar tip for the waiter, Mom."

"Twenty dollars!" she gasped, but peeled a worn twenty-dollar bill from her thin wallet. A credit card took care of the rest of the meal.

"Don't worry about it, Mom," Danny said when he saw her worried glance at the check. "God's going to take care of us from now on!"

His mother looked up at him quickly. "God? When

did you start thinking about God, Danny?"

"Oh—" he was flustered, but Dixie gave him an encouraging glance, so he went on, "I've been thinking that I've been pretty ungrateful. I mean, we've had it rough—what with Dad missing and all—but we're alive—and now we're going to have enough money to take care of us. So I think we ought to thank God for His help."

Mrs. Fortune's eyes filled with tears. She turned away from her children, her shoulders shaking. "Aw, Mom—don't cry!" Danny said.

She turned slowly, her lips trembling. "You looked just like your father when you said that, Danny—and you *sounded* like him too!"

Dixie put her arms around her mother. "Mom, you don't have to worry about me anymore, either. I'm not going to steal ever again. That's all over!"

Her mother stared at her, then laughed shakily. "My goodness—I should have sent you away to visit your great-uncles long ago!"

⚡ ⚡ ⚡

The next morning they all waited eagerly for the mail. For one sickening moment as the mailman fumbled through his bag, Danny was afraid that their relatives had found some scheme to get the check back. Finally, the mailman dug it out and handed it over.

Mrs. Fortune waited until the mailman left. Then, with her children watching her, she opened the letter and stared at the little slip of paper tucked inside. "Ten thousand dollars!" she breathed softly.

They all hurried to the bank to deposit it. "Do you

think we'll be able to stay in our apartment now?" Danny asked.

"Yes," his mother said. "And I won't have to take on a second job, either." She smiled at Dixie. "Do you know what this means, honey? We can finally get you your braces!"

"Oh, there's no hurry, Mom." Dixie shrugged. "It's not urgent."

Her mother stared at her. "But they're all you've talked about for the last two years," she said.

"Well, I guess my priorities were out of order," Dixie admitted uncomfortably. "The first thing we should do is make sure Jimmy keeps getting the right kind of medical care."

They all agreed that Jimmy should visit a specialist who had discovered some encouraging research about cystic fibrosis.

"Dixie and I will have to go see our uncles tomorrow, Mom," Danny interrupted their happy mood.

"Well, you be careful working around that laboratory," she replied seriously. "Those places can be dangerous!"

"Oh, we'll be very careful!" Dixie laughed. "We won't blow ourselves up or anything like that."

Before the twins went to bed that evening, Dixie whispered to Danny, "I took a look in my history book, and I discovered something awful."

"What's that?" he asked.

"Remember Mr. Billington? Well, I thought he was pretty bad in 1620, but he got *worse*! He became involved in a plot to overthrow the government—and in 1630 he had a fight with a man named John Newcomen. Billington ambushed him in a lonely part of the forest and shot him dead!"

"No!" Danny exclaimed. "What did the town do to him?"

"He was the first American to be hanged for a crime," Dixie said. She shuddered at the thought and added, "And Captain Jones died less than a year after the trip. The book said he probably died of the hard times he went through on the voyage to Plymouth."

"He was a good man," Danny said. It felt weird to read in a history book about people they knew so well. "What else did you come across?"

"Oh, John Alden married Priscilla in 1622. They had lots of children and John went on to become an assistant governor of the colony."

"That's no surprise. I liked John—in fact, I liked almost all of them, Saints and Strangers alike," Danny said. "The United States sure wouldn't be the same without them!"

"Well, now, I trust that your dear mother is well?" Mordecai said smoothly as the twins sat down in the great-uncles' study the next day. "After all, Brother Zacharias and I have always had a warm feeling for your father and her."

"Sure you have." Danny nodded. "That's why you rushed to help Mom when Dad disappeared."

Mordecai's face fell.

"Now, now, can't we let bygones be bygones?" Zacharias asked. "After all, we have done a little something to help your family, haven't we now?"

"You're right, Uncle," Dixie admitted. "Let me tell you how much good the money you gave Mom has done." She recited their good news and added, "Thanks, both of you. Your help just about saved our lives—at least Jimmy's."

"Well, that's very generous of you, my dear!" Zacharias said. "And now may we attend to the business at hand?"

"Go ahead," Danny said, waiting for them to begin. The two men were acting strangely—they seemed jumpy and uncomfortable.

Zacharias gave his brother an odd look, and Mordecai nodded at him in an encouraging way.

"As I have said, we were only too glad to help your mother. We fully intend to see to it that she is never reduced to such a sad condition in the future. Of course, if we undertake that, I'm sure you two wouldn't refuse to do a little more scientific work for us—would you now?"

Danny stared at him—he knew what was coming. "You mean you want us to take another trip in the Chrono-Shuttle?"

"Exactly," Zacharias nodded, a smile on his thin lips. "We can't stop *now*, can we? You two aren't scientists, but you must see that we owe it to the world to pursue these experiments. Think what our discoveries will mean to the world!"

"Think what it will mean when something goes wrong and we get stuck in the year one thousand B.C.!" Danny snapped. He got to his feet, his face angry. "I just *knew* you two were up to something. And the answer is no!"

"But why not? Everything worked so beautifully last time!" Zacharias whined.

"That's what you think!" Dixie said angrily. "What if we lose the Recall Unit again? Or what if it doesn't work? There are all kinds of things that can go wrong."

"But the Recall Unit *did* work," Zacharias pointed out. "It worked perfectly—just as I designed it to!"

Danny got to his feet. *I'm not going to put up with these men anymore—not when we don't have to.* "Come on, Dixie. There's no use arguing with these two. We're not going anywhere in the Chrono-Shuttle, and that's the end of it!"

Dixie got up to leave with him, and Mordecai blurted suddenly, "Is this absolutely your *final* answer, Danny?"

"Yes!"

The little man sat down slowly. He looked exhausted. After a long pause, he turned to his brother and said quietly, "We'll have to tell them, Zacharias."

"No! We can't!" his twin shouted.

Danny and Dixie had been headed for the door, but they stopped and turned to face the two men. "Tell us *what*?" Danny asked curiously.

"Don't tell them anything, Mordecai!"

"But I must!" Mordecai insisted. He looked Danny in the eye. "Would you and Dixie please come and sit down. I . . . I have something to tell you. It's important."

Danny and Dixie exchanged glances, then Danny said, "Guess it won't hurt to listen."

"That is where you are wrong, my boy," Mordecai said. "It *is* going to hurt—maybe as much as anything ever hurt you in your whole life."

Suddenly Dixie's face grew white, and her hands started to tremble. "It's about our f-father . . . isn't it?"

"I'm afraid so," Mordecai said sheepishly.

Danny felt as if a door had opened under him and he were falling helplessly. "Is he . . . dead?" he whispered. As soon as he had asked, he wished he hadn't. Saying the word made it seem too real.

"Oh no!" Zacharias said, then quickly added, "We don't think so."

"What is *that* supposed to mean?" Danny exploded.

"Well, as you know, your father did some work for us from time to time," Mordecai looked down at the floor as he spoke, and Zacharias started busily polishing the globe on the table beside him.

"Go on." Danny wished they would get to the point.

"Well . . ." Mordecai hesitated, then said carefully, "The work he did—it was connected with the Chrono-Shuttle."

"What?!" Danny and Dixie shouted in unison.

"You shouldn't have told them, Mordecai!" Zacharias moaned. "A court might find us at fault."

"What do you mean 'at fault'? Just what have you done with our father?" Dixie's eyes sparked.

Zacharias swallowed and said in a high-pitched whisper, "He's somewhere in the past!"

Danny felt a hot pulse of anger rush through his veins. "You sent him to the past like you did us," he said slowly. "But you couldn't get him back again—is that what happened?" He glared accusingly at his twin great-uncles.

"Unfortunately . . . yes," Zacharias yanked a large handkerchief from his pocket and mopped his shiny forehead. "That's one of the main reasons why we wanted you to travel back in time. You see, I've only just developed the Recall Unit you used this last week. And now that we know it's a success . . ."

"Wait a minute. Are you saying all we have to do is go back in the past, find my father, and get him out with the Recall Unit?"

Mordecai nodded, a relieved look on his face. "That is the plan. And that is precisely why you must go back! You must find him and bring him back!"

"Why didn't you say so in the first place?" Danny asked. "Of course I'll go! I'll go right now! What year is he in?"

Zacharias coughed slightly, cast a fearful look at his brother, and said with a great deal of hesitation, "That is where the problem lies."

"I don't see any problem," Danny argued. "Just send me to the year and the place he traveled to. I'll have him back in no time."

Zacharias still hesitated, and Dixie cried out, "You don't know where he is, do you?"

"N-not *exactly*," the scientist admitted uneasily.

"Well, if not *exactly*, how about *approximately*!" Danny snapped.

"He's sometime between the year 1620 and . . . and—"

"And *what*!" Dixie was yelling.

"Well, between then and 1861," Zacharias finally said. Then he began speaking very rapidly, "Now wait! It's not as bad as it sounds. Your father agreed to travel to the past—what historian wouldn't, you know—but he insisted on choosing the time. He talked about it a great deal, sometimes wanting to go back to the Civil War, then deciding that it would be more exciting to visit the

American Revolution or the Pilgrims and the *May-flower*."

"In the end," Mordecai broke in, "he'd selected twenty possible destinations. I went over them with him many times."

"Well, didn't he tell you which one he'd picked?" Danny asked.

"No, he didn't," Mordecai said in a grieved tone. "He grew impatient. Zacharias was working on a new Recall Unit because he was afraid the original one was too weak. So one night your father came to the Chrono-Shuttle, got in, and sent himself back in time. He rigged the control panel."

"Didn't he leave a note?" Dixie asked.

"Yes, but he forgot to say which time he'd chosen—only that it was the one we'd talked about," Mordecai said. "But we'd talked about so many! I don't have the faintest idea which one he chose—except that it wasn't 1620. That was the choice I thought was most likely. But if he had chosen that, he'd have been on the *Mayflower*! Obviously you would have run into him."

"He's got to know we're trying desperately to get him back," Zacharias added. "Wherever he is, he'll be expecting someone to come now that he knows his Recall Unit doesn't work. He'll know to get involved in the most famous historical event of that time—that's what we'll be looking for."

"Let's see the list," Danny said. Mordecai went to a desk and returned with a small sheet of paper. "Here it is—he wrote it himself."

Dixie leaned in to read the list. The sight of their father's handwriting brought a lump to Danny's throat. "We've got to go find him!" Dixie whispered. "He must be feeling so lost out there! I'm sure he's worried sick about us and how we're doing without him."

Danny reread the list, then looked at Mordecai. "What time do you think he picked? I know it'll be just a *guess*."

Mordecai tugged his beard nervously, then shook his head. "He talked a lot about the young George Washington and his involvement in the French and Indian War. He was very interested in that period."

"Well," Danny said, "I'm afraid I don't know much about that war."

"It isn't very well known, I'll admit. But your father talked about it all the time."

"It sounds like a good bet," Dixie said. "We'll have to try it."

"It could be very dangerous!" Mordecai warned. "The Indians raided the farms in the Ohio Valley and killed every white person they found."

"How soon can we leave?" Dixie asked quietly.

Mordecai stared at the two. "You'll need some quick briefing from an expert—me, I suppose. Let's say tomorrow after school. You will have to know how to behave and how to talk."

"All right. It sounds like a plan to me," Danny said. Dixie nodded her agreement.

Mordecai began the briefing as he and Zacharias drove the twins home. As Danny and Dixie got out of the old black Cadillac and watched it pull away, Dixie asked, "Should we tell Mom?"

Danny shook his head. "I don't think so, Dixie. We don't want to get her hopes up. This could take a long time." *But at least now we can do something,* Danny added silently.

"Wouldn't it be great if we found Dad right away—just brought him back and walked into the apartment with him?" Dixie's eyes glowed at the thought.

"It sure would be a miracle," Danny said with a smile. "But I guess we learned that much from the Pilgrims, didn't we? How to trust God for miracles?"

"Sure! What's a little miracle to God?" Dixie laughed.

They bounced up the stairs, stopping for a moment at the top. "Maybe tomorrow night, Dixie, Dad will be coming up these stairs with us."

Dixie gave him a quick hug and a bright smile.

"Mom, we're home!" Danny called, and he raced into the shabby apartment with a smile.

DATE DUE			
SEP. 27			

Morris, Gilbert

The Dangerous Voyage

GAYLORD M2